LAST SPELL

EMMA LAST SERIES: BOOK TWELVE

MARY STONE

Copyright © 2025 by Mary Stone Publishing

All rights reserved.

No part of this book may be reproduced in any form or by any electronic or mechanical means, including information storage and retrieval systems, without written permission from the author, except for the use of brief quotations in a book review.

❦ Created with Vellum

To the readers who have given me the space to explore the mysterious. Your support has allowed me to dip my toe into the supernatural, something I've always loved, and for that, I am endlessly grateful. Thank you for going on this journey with me.

LETTER FROM THE AUTHOR

Dear Beloved Readers,

Before I was even a teen, I remember staying up late reading Stephen King, devouring stories that blurred the lines between reality and the supernatural. Those tales left me wondering what might be knocking at the door when the wind howls at night, a curiosity that has never quite left me.

Over the years, I've rooted my stories more firmly in the terrors of reality, focusing on the darkness humanity is capable of. But with Emma Last, I've always left a crack in the door for the unexplained. After all, she's already seen ghosts—things she can't rationalize or fit into the neat categories of evidence and motive.

This book takes Emma further into the unknown. Spells, mind control, and forces she cannot see test her in ways no crime scene ever could. It's a leap, and I'll admit, a bit of a risk, but one I've loved taking. A leap I wouldn't have been brave enough to take without your enduring support.

For those of you who have followed Emma's journey, I hope you enjoy this deeper dive into the mysterious and supernatural. And for those who may be skeptical of this shift, I promise Emma's core—her resilience, her humanity, her drive for justice—remains unchanged.

Thank you for joining me on this adventure. Your support means the world, and I hope this story leaves you wondering, as I always do, about what might really be knocking at the door.

With love, gratitude, and more than a little curiosity,
　Mary

DESCRIPTION

Curse the darkness. Or embrace it. There's no other choice.

Special Agent Emma Last barely survived the psychic attack that tore through her when she drove past her hometown of Salem for a case. At the time, she was chasing a cannibal through a booby-trapped wilderness, but the shadows of Salem have lingered, haunting her every mile.

Now, she's not just driving past—she's going back. On purpose.

Emma and two of her closest colleagues arrive to assist with a puzzling crime wave plaguing Salem. Four unrelated arsons, over a dozen muggings, vandalism, carjacking, home invasions. Every crime has been committed by a person with no criminal background. Stranger still, none remember their crimes.

Emma knows something sinister and supernatural is at play.

Her late mother's two best friends each blame the other for using magic to manipulate the people of Salem into acts of violence. But as the attacks escalate to murder, Emma uncovers a chilling truth. One of the women deliberately lured Emma to Salem to kill her.

But which one?

Fighting a threat she can't see and unsure who she can trust, Emma must find the source of the madness destroying Salem. Before it destroys her.

Last Spell, the twelfth book in the Emma Last FBI series by bestselling author Mary Stone, will make you curse the day you were born. Or wonder if someone else did.

1

Phoebe Wilson settled into her electronic recliner and sighed. Heat from the newfangled contraption's warmer soothed her lower back. Such a minor bit of comfort, but she needed it for her nightly ritual of watching the nine o'clock news.

Though why she bothered...

"What's Salem coming to? I just don't know." The camera view expanded to show crime scene tape surrounding a path in Arrowhead Park. Phoebe used to walk her late poodle, Miss Fluffkin, through that very stretch. "Oh, Miss Fluffs, if you could see what's happened to the world."

Muggings at gunpoint. Robberies. Family members attacking each other. Murders and arsons, even. Violence at every turn. It seemed the only thing reporters covered now. It also gave her a serious case of the creepy-crawlies every night when she sat down in her chair. Her back was to the front room windows.

Even with the curtains drawn, she couldn't shake the feeling of being watched, and she worried about someone throwing something through the window.

"Nothing but bad, bad, bad, and it makes you think the worst." She frowned at the television, adjusting her glasses. Maybe she'd write a letter. Ask them to cover something happy for a change. "That's silly, Phoebe Wilson, and you know it. Who's going to listen to an eighty-four-year-old woman with a quivery voice?" She used to have a voice that carried, back when she was a schoolteacher.

I'm glad my dear Albert isn't here to see me like this. I suppose I could've called Howard earlier and asked him to come by. We could play chess or do a crossword.

Howard Blackwood was a neighbor a few streets over. Since Albert had died, Howard had been coming around to make sure Phoebe wasn't lonely or in need of anything.

He wasn't the only gentleman who offered support, but he certainly was the kindest.

A knock interrupted the reporter, who was still rambling on about violence.

"At this time of night? Too late for those blasted solar panel salespeople."

Whoever it was, they knocked again—and hard. Four pounds of a fist. Phoebe's heart sped up. Had violence found its way to her door?

She levered herself forward and turned sideways toward the chair Albert used to sit in. She'd left it where it was, unable to move it herself and seeing no reason why she should.

When Albert was alive, that was his spot to watch television. And if anyone knocked on the door, he'd just flick the curtain aside to see who it was.

Now Phoebe struggled to see through the slim gap between the curtains. She got a glimpse of red hair as the person shifted back and forth.

Looks like Damien. Wonder what's gotten a bee in his bonnet this time of night.

Her neighbor from two doors down had been an even bigger help than Howard, if Phoebe was being honest.

Howard was great for fun and games, but he was too old to push a lawn mower or haul the garbage cans up and down the driveway on trash days.

Damien could do that for her, and he never asked for much in return, though she did counsel him about wearing sunscreen when he mowed her lawn.

The poor man's pale as a ghost, and that red hair means he's at risk of skin cancer.

Damien might not have had the most receptive ears for her motherly advice, but Phoebe still thought he was sweet, a lot like the son she and Albert raised.

He knocked again, louder this time.

"Hold your horses, Damien! I'm coming!"

She pushed the button on her chair and waited for the footrest to lower her legs. When her feet hit the floor, she took care to stand so she wouldn't lose her balance.

If she had to have a late visitor, Damien Knight wasn't a bad one. He'd probably gotten it in his head to worry about her over something, or maybe he finally met the right woman and was here to tell her he was getting married.

At the front door, she peered through the peephole to be sure it was him. Used to be, she hadn't even kept this door locked, but things had changed in Salem.

She took in his brawny physique, which might've looked intimidating to some, but the boy was a gentle giant. Bushy red hair and a thick beard gave him a teddy bear aura.

There was no good reason he was still single.

"Hang on. Give an old woman a second!" She worked at the dead bolt, wondering if she should ask him in for some tea. She'd just see what he wanted to tell her first. Could be he was just there to say she'd forgotten to take her mail in again.

Opening the door, she leaned against it and squinted at the young man before her.

Something felt off. A sinister vibe rolled off him, but she couldn't put her finger on what the change was. He kept his eyes directed toward his feet. She took a step back before she stopped herself.

It's Damien. Calm down.

But his eyes were focused on something beyond her, and he had his fist raised to knock again. He mumbled something about spirits. Clearly, he was in his cups. Hopefully, it was only alcohol.

Maybe he met the wrong woman and is just drowning his sorrows.

His mouth moved and sounds escaped, but his voice was little more than a mutter. She couldn't make out a word of it.

"Damien, what's wrong? Your words are getting lost in that beard of yours."

He worked his lips, finally dropping his fist, but it remained clenched. Finally, he looked at her…or, rather, toward her.

His normally warm brown eyes were now a haunting, featureless white. Devoid of irises, they reflected nothing but a strange emptiness.

She blinked. It had to be the light. She wasn't seeing things right.

Damien looked down again, and Phoebe convinced herself she was imagining the whole scenario.

"It's a pact, Phoebe," he finally got out. "Me, the spirits, and her." He swayed where he stood, and Phoebe's heart ached for him.

"Damien, you poor soul. You know drink won't solve your girl problems."

When he lifted his strange white eyes from the floor to her face, she staggered back, gripping the door for support.

Whatever had gotten to him tonight, it wasn't grief, and it wasn't alcohol.

"You're on something. You need a doctor." She kept her voice low, gentle, but channeled all her teaching years into it. "You go on home now. It's too late to be bothering an old woman. You can come over for tea tomorrow."

Damien's arm shot out in front of him, blocking the closing door.

"What are you doing?" Phoebe fell backward, catching herself on the entryway table. The little dish Albert always put his keys in crashed to the floor, sending fragments of ceramic in every direction. "Damien!"

He pushed inside and loomed over her. His mouth gaped like a ventriloquist's dummy, and his eyes were truly and decidedly all white. Not a single sign of his warm brown irises remained.

"What's happened?" Her throat was dry, and her voice cracked. She put one hand on her chest, willing her heart to slow down. "What did you take? I'll call poison control."

His meaty hand came up and hovered between them. She couldn't take her eyes off it. The limb appeared to hang in the air as, one by one, his fingers stretched out toward her like the legs of a spider.

"What's going on? You're scaring me."

His hand shot forward, catching her around the neck. She gulped against it, fighting for air just as his other paw came up to anchor her against the wall.

She gripped at his forearms and tore at his fingers, trying to speak a single word that might get through to him.

He lifted her from the floor. Her feet beat against the wall as something in her neck cracked and heat shot down her spine.

She couldn't breathe. Her lungs were going to explode.

No matter how wide her mouth opened, how she fought him, not a touch of air reached them.

His hands were like steel cords around her neck as she dangled in his grip.

This isn't Damien. He wouldn't do this. He...

The thought dissolved with her breath. Frozen in a silent scream, she stared into his empty eyes, her pleas for mercy swallowed by the darkness around her.

2

FBI Special Agent Emma Last never expected the trip to Salem to be short, but it was taking about three times as long as it should've, given her partner in law enforcement, Leo Ambrose, had insisted on driving. Special Agent Mia Logan had seemed happy to let him take the wheel. Emma supposed she couldn't blame her friends and colleagues. She drove like a maniac at the best of times, and this was not the best of times.

Salem was Emma's hometown. But last time she'd recently driven through it—on the way to Boston for another case with Leo—she'd been overcome by a gripping sensation that threatened to crush her. Ice-cold tendrils had raced up and down her spine and through her body, locking her in their grasp.

And that had happened as they drove past the city, never leaving the freeway. Today, they were heading into the heart of Salem.

Their exit was coming up in a mile. So far, she'd only experienced mild chills…nothing so traumatic as last time.

Mia gripped Emma's shoulder, giving her a squeeze.

When Emma twisted in her seat to glance back at her friend and fellow agent, Mia offered her a hesitant smile.

"You looked tense. It'll be okay. We're here, and we'll figure things out together."

On the surface, their reasons for heading into Salem sounded ridiculous. Esther, a fortune teller whose ex-husband had been involved in their previous case, had told her that *"Salem will run red with blood."*

Only this past week, their Violent Crime Unit had resolved a particularly heinous case involving a cannibal who had set up booby traps in the wilderness to ensnare his victims. While they'd been too late to save Esther's husband, they'd managed to save her son.

"According to these police reports, our fortune teller friend is right." Mia leaned forward from the back seat and held up her tablet so Emma could see. "Salem's going through quite the crime wave."

Emma scanned reports and newspaper headlines, her breath catching in her throat as she read about the recent uptick of violent crimes. "Listen to this. 'The Truth behind Salem's Unprecedented Rising Crime Rate.' 'Where Are Police amid Crime Wave?' And a favorite here, 'Salem Prefers Hauntings over Real Terror.'"

Mia huffed. "The way the papers talk, you'd think we'd have been hearing about it all the way in DC. Was it really that quiet here before?"

Emma scrolled through the reports. "When I was growing up, it was. Now it sounds more like Gotham City. Four unrelated arsons last month? Over a dozen muggings in broad daylight. Vandalism, carjacking, home invasions…"

"That's a lot of violent crime." Leo glanced over.

Emma pointed at the windshield. "Eyes on the road, grandpa."

With a huff, Leo looked back out the windshield.

She gestured at the tablet. "You're not kidding. Looks like a lot of these were committed by people without any prior criminal background too."

Mia inhaled sharply as she pulled up the most recent report. "Did you see what happened last night?"

Emma took the tablet back and read the report out loud. "'A woman in her eighties, Phoebe Wilson, was allegedly murdered by her longtime neighbor, Damien Knight, who was known to help with yard work, groceries, and other household chores. The suspect had no prior history of criminal behavior, and other neighbors described him as extremely kind.'"

Damien Knight's mug shot showed a young man who looked more confused than malevolent.

A chill ran down Emma's spine, but this had nothing to do with the Other changing temperatures on her. She shivered and handed the tablet back to Mia.

"You good? Is it the cold again?"

"No. I'm fine. A few little chills, but not like last time. I think something or someone is getting in the way."

Mia had known Emma could see ghosts for a few months now. But the newest twist on her ability had happened during their previous case. She'd been overwhelmed by the Other while entering their killer's shack in the woods.

Emma had passed out, and when she'd come to, she'd been in the Other with a woman who claimed to be a friend of her mother's. The woman introduced herself as Monique Varley.

While in the Other, Monique told Emma she'd placed a protective spell on her before she was born, which would last as long as Monique herself was alive. She also warned Emma that another old friend of her mother's would try to remove the protective ward. Emma could only assume she meant to kill her.

When their case wrapped up, Emma knew she needed to come to Salem, and the escalation of violence in the city strengthened her resolve. As they approached the city limits, she sensed a supernatural element swirling around them, raising the question yet again if the escalation was connected to Emma's personal history.

A freezing wind raised instant goose bumps on her arms, overwhelming her. Emma jerked back in her seat, tugging down the sleeves of her button-down.

Leo clearly saw her trembling. "Hotel's on the other side of the city. Want me to stop and get you a winter coat?"

"Ha." Emma hugged herself to keep warm. "Maybe we could swing past my parents' house, and I'll grab one of Dad's old sweaters."

"You're kidding. You have a house here in Salem that you never told us about?"

"Yeah, over near the Salem State campus, a gated community."

Her friends just nodded. They were kind enough not to make remarks about silver spoons, one more reason that Emma took comfort in their presence. Growing up, everyone who knew about her home life had to make some joke or sarcastic remark.

Another chill racked her body, but as Leo moved toward a stoplight on Salem's main drag, the cold receded.

He cocked his head toward her. "Same as last time?"

Emma swallowed, nodding. "Not as bad. It's been hitting in waves, but…"

"This isn't natural, Emma. I'm worried about you." Mia's voice was shaky. "Can't we at least throw a coat over you or something?"

"I appreciate the thought, but that won't change anything. None of this is natural." She met Mia's gaze in the rearview mirror. "Which is why I can't tell the two of you how much I appreciate you being here for me."

"Hush." Mia squeezed her shoulder again. "But I hate seeing you shivering like this."

As they traveled farther into the city center, the normal trickle of occasional ghosts multiplied. It was as if the floodgates of the Other opened wide, and into this world, they rushed. Denizens were visible to her *everywhere*. Some of the ghosts wore contemporary clothing, possibly victims of the newest crime wave.

I don't know if they have anything to do with what Esther was talking about.

Emma had first met Esther in January, at the circus where Esther worked, when she warned Emma about wolves and blood. Esther's most recent predictions had been more specific and far more unsettling.

"The streets of Salem will run red with blood." She had ended her prophetic mutterings by claiming Salem was *"only the beginning."*

Suppressing another shiver, Emma focused on the ghosts she was seeing now, looking for anything that might help her understand what was happening in her hometown. "Just so you two know, there are lots of ghosts here." She watched as an armless ghost, with blood pouring from its severed shoulder joints, sauntered by between lanes. "Like, everywhere."

Mia raised one eyebrow. "More than in DC?"

Emma stared straight ahead. "Way more."

As they kept driving, she described what she saw. Wounds and clothing ranging from the twenty-first century all the way back to the seventeenth or sixteenth centuries. The spirits were more plentiful than the living. Men with gunshot wounds, women beaten bloody, a few with strangulation marks, and more with gruesome wounds

Emma could only imagine had been caused by serious lunatics or industrial accidents.

When a ghost with catastrophic burn scars ran ahead of their car, naked and screaming, Emma stopped narrating the scene and pulled out her own tablet.

"Looks like you're not as cold now, though?" Mia rubbed her shoulder, then sat back in her seat as Leo continued to edge them through the stop-and-go traffic.

Emma kept her focus on the tablet. "It's better now that we've left the freeway. I'm just glad Jacinda gave us time off." She turned and smiled at Mia, then Leo. "Seriously, it means a lot that you two are here instead of taking some well-deserved rest. That's more than anyone could ask of you after days spent fighting a real-life cannibal and escaping those woods. Nobody would've blamed you if you'd wanted to retreat to a spa or just lay in bed for a week. Least of all me."

"This is too important for us to put off, what with the way it's been affecting you." Leo took another turn, following the dashboard GPS. "Like we said, we're here for you. And hell, after we faced a wild Hannibal Lecter, the least the Bureau could do is give us some therapeutic leave."

Mia smirked at Emma via the rearview mirror. "And it's none of their business if we use it to, um, do more work." She waved her tablet, rotating the Salem crime reports to vertical on-screen, then horizontal, then back again. "Or handle your ghosts."

Emma relaxed her shoulders. Her body was warming up again. "We have to talk to Monique Varley face-to-face. Get the full story. Because I'm still not sure she can be trusted."

Whatever was happening in Salem, they had to get to the bottom of it. If the crime wave and the ghosts were tied to Emma, they might be the only ones in a position to help.

Leo extended his right hand for a fist bump. "All for one."
Emma and Mia met his fist with theirs. "And one for all."

3

Once they'd checked into the hotel, Emma sat on the floor, against the foot of her bed, in a meditation posture that her late boyfriend had taught her. She did her best to channel Oren's calming essence, but thinking of him and his death still hurt. And Emma would never be free of the memories.

Oren dead on the floor of his studio.
His blood pooling around his gunshot wound.
Leo calling her away from his lifeless form.

Pushing aside those images and calling up better ones, like Oren's laugh and his yoga lessons, Emma focused on breathing deep and evenly.

In and out. In and out.

Maybe she'd technically met one of the women from her mom's photo via those visions last week, but that had been in the world of the Other. Today's meeting would be *in person*, in the land of the living, and that felt big. Whether she could trust Monique was still in question.

But if those women in the photograph had been as close to Emma's mother as she suspected, shouldn't that mean they'd be like family?

The closest thing I have to family anyway. They knew me when I was born and might know intimate details about my mom's connection to the Other.

But can I trust them? Either of them?

As if in response to the unspoken question, a sharp and sudden knock, very similar to what Emma thought of as a cop's knock, assaulted her door.

She peered through the peephole with the expectation of seeing one of her colleagues, though she'd have expected Leo or Mia to call out or use their off-duty knock.

Instead, the other woman in her mother's photograph—the one who wasn't Monique—stared back at her. Her hair was silvery white, pulled back into an efficient French twist. But otherwise, she looked the same. Her smooth, lightly tanned skin was without blemish. Her brown eyes glittered, keen and intelligent. She wore a navy blue pantsuit with a crisp white blouse. And, if Emma saw it correctly through the distorted fish-eye lens of the peephole, a badge hung from her belt.

She's a cop.

She's also the woman Monique warned you about. But is that because she's dangerous or because Monique is? Watch your step, Emma girl.

Emma took a breath and opened the door.

The woman's eyes widened. "Gi...?" She cut herself off. "No. Of course not. Apologies. You're Emma Last. It's about time we met. I'm Celeste Foss. You've heard of me?" She smiled again, the expression sharp and thin in a way that made her look more serious than friendly.

Now that Emma was face-to-face with Celeste, she felt torn by time—between the past that belonged to her mother and her own present-moment existence—but she nodded and stepped forward, trying for a casual air as she leaned against the doorframe of her hotel room. "I'm sorry. I haven't heard of you."

Celeste's face fell ever so slightly. "That's...disappointing. Your mother and I were very close."

"I've seen your picture, at least." Emma didn't understand the impulse to make this woman, this stranger, feel better, but she tried. "I have a photograph of you, with my mother and another woman."

Celeste's smile remained frozen on her face as she tilted her head. "Monique Varley. Yes. I believe you've been in contact with her as well?"

You have both of their names now. I suppose that's something. And Celeste knows Monique found you in the Other or suspects that to be true.

Emma took a beat before answering, hearing the woman's voice shift to a subtle interrogating tone. The cop was peeking through. "Briefly." Emma shrugged. "I was hoping to run into both of you this weekend. I felt the need to come back to Salem. Get back to my roots."

"It *is* where you were born. One's place of power, as it were."

"How did you know I was here?" Emma repeated the woman's turn of phrase in her mind, to mark down later. Was Salem her "place of power?" And, if so, what did that mean?

Celeste gave her a knowing look. "You're not the only one who can see into the Other, my girl. At the risk of sounding like a prophetess, I sensed you coming. When the request for Salem's most recent crime reports came in from your partner, Special Agent Mia Logan, I was the one who approved sharing them. I hope you'll help me."

Emma felt like a scolded child for some reason. "Well, I'm here." She drew the door a bit closer behind her, not wanting Celeste to invite herself inside. She felt the need to keep a bit of distance until she could figure out which of her mother's old friends to trust. "I've been reading about the violence in Salem, and it does seem like the authorities here could use some help."

"Oh, it's all horrible, isn't it?" Celeste's eyes flashed with a bit of righteous anger. "Salem isn't what it used to be when your mother and I were friends. I'm afraid Monique might be playing a role in the whole thing."

Emma's fingers tightened on the handle. "How and why do you think Monique's involved?"

Celeste's lips curled. "I've known her for a very long time. I've seen some dark things, my girl. As have you, I imagine. We have that in common."

The air thickened, as Emma was accustomed to when the Other intruded on her space, but no ghost appeared. She was in the presence of some power she couldn't quite figure out, though. Perhaps it was just being so close to someone who might understand what she'd gone through.

Don't trust her. Don't trust anyone yet.

"If you don't mind, Celeste, I'd love to know why you're here, exactly. You show up out of the blue when I haven't even contacted you."

"Oh, don't be like that." Celeste tilted her head, a smile widening her mouth. "My girl, don't be so suspicious. It's not rocket science. You're a darling of the FBI. All anyone has to do is search your name to know that Gina hatched a smart, gorgeous creature who serves justice like a superhero, and Salem should be glad you've graced us with your presence. I know I am. I'm at my wit's end. But I won't force your hand."

She reached into her pocket and pulled out a business card. The Salem Police Department logo dominated one side. On the other, *Detective Celeste Foss, Homicide* and a series of contact numbers and a website were embossed.

"If you have time, I'd love for you and your colleagues to

stop by the station." She handed the card over. "If you plan to speak to Monique Varley, then be on your guard. She's always been a manipulative liar. Whatever she's told you, or whatever she's going to tell you, you mustn't believe her. It's likely a trap."

A chill swept through Emma just before a tired-looking ghost in a suit strolled around the corner and down her corridor. He passed just behind Celeste, muttering under his breath. "Liar, liar. Pants on fire."

No way to tell if he was talking about Celeste or confirming what she'd said about Monique.

Lovely.

Emma studied Celeste's placid face. "But I should believe you instead? You must know how that sounds very *she said, she said.*"

"The consequences of not believing me are deadly. Believing in lies so often can be." Celeste held Emma's gaze, forcing her to recognize the same powerful expression from that old photograph. This woman was probably amazing at interrogations.

Emma's guts churned with indecision, a sensation she was generally unfamiliar with. Monique had reached through the Other and pulled Emma out of a dangerous case to talk to her, yanking her from her own reality and leaving her helpless. If it hadn't been for Leo and Mia, she might've ended up a victim of the cannibal they'd been hunting through the Buckskin wilderness.

And for what? The only thing Monique had really done was insist that Emma come visit her in Salem, and she'd encouraged her to be wary of Celeste. She hadn't named the woman, but Emma's conversation with Monique revolved around "her mother's old friends."

What had Celeste done, beyond knocking on a hotel room door and asking for her help to solve crimes?

Celeste extended her hand.

Emma took it, and the two women shook, but Celeste didn't immediately let go.

"I imagine Monique is planning to destroy the spell of protection I placed on you at your birth." She smiled, though there was no humor or joy in it. "But know the only way to destroy a protective spell is to destroy the caster. You mustn't let that happen."

Emma's eyes widened, despite her best attempts to avoid it. Now the women were directly contradicting each other. "You placed the protective spell on me?"

"Ah." Celeste nodded to herself as she let Emma's hand go. "Monique claimed credit, didn't she? I should've known."

The woman shook her head, either deeply disheartened by the news or pretending to be.

"Emma, dear, she's trying to put one over on you. I cast a spell of protection that helped you leave Salem until you were old enough to come back and face Monique. *Prepared enough.*" She leaned in so close that Emma breathed in her musky perfume. "And if the two of us work together now, we can stop her. We can save lives across Salem. Just like your mother would've wanted."

Emma's heart thumped against her ribs. "I appreciate the offer. I think I need to determine who to trust on my own first. I'm sure you understand."

"There isn't a great deal of time." Celeste's eyes narrowed to two slits. "I hope you'll consider your options quickly. I'll be at the station if you need me." She turned and made her way back toward the stairwell. The cold retreated with her.

Emma waited until Celeste Foss had disappeared from view before stepping over to the door next to hers and knocking.

"What's going on?"

She didn't answer Mia's question but, instead, grabbed

her hand and led her to Leo's door. They knocked, and Leo opened his door almost instantaneously.

The two of them ducked into his room.

Emma's pulse continued to hammer inside her, but at least her voice remained steady when she spoke. "You'll never guess who just showed up at my doorway. The *other* woman in my mom's photo, Celeste Foss." She held up the business card. "*Detective* Celeste Foss."

Leo's eyebrows rose. "I take it she didn't attack you?"

Emma snorted a laugh. "No, but she did tell me that *she* was the one who cast the protective spell on me, not Monique, and that she believes Monique is luring us to her home to kill me."

Mia plopped down on the spare bed in Leo's room. "So you have two of your mom's old friends…each claiming the other wants you dead and each one saying they've been protecting you all these years." She offered a small, crooked grin. "Could your life get any more complicated?"

"Dang, I hope not." Leo frowned. "What do you want to do?"

Emma shook her head. "I don't think anything's changed. I can't really trust either one of them, cop or not. Monique endangered me by drawing me into the Other like she did, and there's something cold about Celeste. But she does want investigative help with the crime wave in Salem right now, so there's that too."

"Wouldn't that put one tick in the *Trust Celeste* column?" Leo crossed his arms.

"Maybe. But it could be part of her setup. And according to Celeste, the only way to stop a protective spell is to kill the person who cast it. She may want to use us to get close to Monique."

"Or Monique may want to use us to get close to Celeste." Leo frowned.

"So we stick with the plan." Mia stood and pushed her pant legs back down. "Or do you want one of us to hang back, just in case?"

Before Emma had a chance to consider the option, Leo help up a hand. "No, we stick together. If there were four of us, maybe we'd split into teams of two, but as things stand, we need to stick together on this."

Much as Emma was terrified of drawing them into danger, that did seem safest. "I agree. Maybe after we see Monique, it'll be clearer what's what. And we stay on our guard anyway."

Leo gave a tight nod, his frown as deep as Emma had ever seen it.

4

After Leo and Mia asked all the questions Emma would allow, they agreed to go ahead with meeting Monique. Before setting out, with the car's key fob tucked into his pocket, Leo took a moment to himself outside while Emma and Mia grabbed coffee and bagels from the café next door.

Without really knowing who they could trust in Salem—and feeling certain that this would all get worse before it got better—Leo had to talk with Denae, who was still recovering from a gunshot wound.

Her doctor said she could be released from the hospital in as few as five days. She was responding well, he'd heard, but they hadn't communicated since her email earlier in the week.

And that only came through because Jamaal typed it for her while she dictated. She's going to be fine. She's alive and...

He knew better than to even think that things might go back to normal between them. Her email had said as much.

"I need to spend some time healing and also focusing on my family."

That didn't mean he couldn't call and wish her well. This

might be his last chance to hear her voice before things went south here in Salem.

Assuming she's able to talk. Or that she wants to.

He placed the call, and a nurse answered. "Ms. Monroe is awake, yes. She has PT scheduled in about ten minutes, but I'll put you through to her room."

Leo waited, his heart thudding as hold music came through the line. He ran through all the things he wanted to say, and the things he knew not to say. And the things he wished he'd said a hundred times before.

Her voice interrupted his jumbled mind. "Hi, Leo."

A deep ache ran through him at the sound of his name. "Denae. It's so good to hear your voice."

The pause that followed lingered a little too long. "Yours too. What's happening out there in the real world?"

There it was, that straightforward attitude he loved so much. "I'm in Salem with Emma and Mia. Just wanted to call before…" He couldn't tell her why they'd come, not really. But he couldn't lie to her either.

"Before?"

"We're here for Emma. She's digging into her family history. Mia and I came along for emotional support."

Another long pause. "She's grateful for that, I'm sure." He heard her hesitation from hundreds of miles away. "Leo, listen. Emma's situation is complicated."

That's the understatement of the year. His gut twisted.

"What do you mean by 'complicated?'" He sounded so phony, even to himself. Denae would see through him in a heartbeat.

"I saw her, when I was in the coma. I mean…I didn't *see her*, see her. But I did. Every now and then. We were in, like, a parallel world thing? I was standing over myself, and she was there too."

He waited her out, his heart picking up speed. Denae had been in the Other. She'd seen Emma and remembered.

"I sound insane."

Leo opened his mouth to tell her no, to spill everything he knew. "I—"

"Listen, I gotta go, Leo. PT is in a few minutes. Just…be careful with Emma."

"Do you think I shouldn't help her?"

"No." She was direct and emphatic. "You *need* to help her. But that help might be…complicated. That place, this netherworld or in-between space where I saw her, was cold and creepy. I'm not making any of that up. I'm fine."

The fatigue in her voice overshadowed any of the vigor he'd initially sensed, and he realized her straightforwardness was more likely an effort at sounding normal again. She didn't want him worrying over her.

That wouldn't stop him from doing it, but he could respect her needs just the same.

"Yeah, the nurse said you had that PT coming up. It's…it was good talking with you, even for a little bit. For what it's worth, I believe you. About Emma."

"Thanks for calling, Scruffy."

She ended the call, and Leo stuffed his phone in his pocket, not wanting to see her name wink out on the screen.

By the time Emma and Mia came back with breakfast, he was in the driver's seat with the engine running. His eyes were mostly dry and hidden behind his sunglasses.

If either of them noticed, they didn't say anything.

Leo took a sip of coffee, the warmth of the engine doing little to soothe the cold unease clinging to him. His pulse thrummed, his thoughts spiraling as Emma and Mia chatted quietly. He'd been trying to wrap his head around everything—ghosts, possession, Salem—ever since Emma first told him about her family's connection to the Other.

The truth was, he'd never ruled out the possibility of ghosts, or aliens, or the paranormal—any of it. He didn't believe it, exactly. But he couldn't dismiss it either. The universe was too vast, too strange, for humanity to have everything figured out.

Still, this was different. Emma didn't just believe in ghosts —she *saw* them, interacted with them. And here he was, preparing to trek through haunted woods with someone who casually pointed out invisible entities like they were street signs. It made him want to be open-minded, to support her. He owed her that much. But deep down, he wondered how much of himself he was willing to bend before he broke.

Is this what losing my mind feels like?

Maybe the pressure of everything—the cases, Denae, this —was finally catching up to him. Or maybe he was just afraid of admitting that Emma's world was starting to bleed into his own.

Emma wiped her mouth, glancing at him. "You okay? You're quiet."

He was prepared to lie, to tell her he was just fine, but the truth slipped out instead. "Just trying to wrap my head around...all of this. Ghosts. Possession. Whatever the hell we're walking into. You know I've never exactly been a skeptic, but I don't always fully believe either."

Emma's gaze lingered on him, steady and unreadable. "Belief isn't always a choice. Sometimes it finds you."

Mia snorted softly. "Like religion?"

Leo took another sip of coffee. "Faith's not so different, is it? You're asked to believe in something you can't see or touch, just trust that it's real. Maybe I've been more open to the idea than I realized. Doesn't make it easier to face when it's right in front of you."

Emma tore off a section of bagel. "If it helps, I'm still figuring out what I believe too."

Somehow, her honesty helped. Leo wasn't sure what scared him more...the idea that ghosts and possession were real or the possibility he was losing his grip on reality. Either way, the line between belief and madness was feeling thinner by the minute.

They'd barely finished the bagels and coffee before reaching Monique Varley's neighborhood that bordered the wilderness preserve she'd noted as her hideaway.

Driving down a street lined with houses, they came to an access road leading into the public area of the wetlands. Narrow driveways led away from the road here and there where private land abutted the preserve.

Leo drove along, following several turns and switchback routes through the wetlands and driving very slowly, even for him. They bounced and jostled in their seats as he navigated the rutted gravel roadway, finally pulling to a stop beside a rusted gate covered in flaking green paint.

Emma checked the notes she'd made from memories of her conversation with Monique. "That's the gate. She said to park outside and walk in."

They got out and stepped around the gateposts, as no fence existed on either side of the standalone feature. But the roadway was the only firm ground visible. Any vehicle attempting to go around the gate would become stuck in seconds.

"Well, that's weird."

Leo didn't comment on Emma's understatement.

A screen of dense trees blocked the view of what lay ahead, where the road curved to the left.

Mia sighed. "I'd never have predicted I'd be walking back into a forest this soon."

By way of answer, Leo forged ahead, scanning the tree line for movement and checking the ground for trip wires or other evidence of traps, just as they'd done on their last case.

It occurred to him they might also be facing threats he couldn't see, no matter how hard they tried, especially if Monique turned out to be the villain in this whole weird scenario. He slowed his pace to fall in step with Emma. "See…anything? Or anybody?"

She shook her head. "Not yet, but the Other is here. I can feel it."

Mia stayed behind them both as they entered the wooded area. The canopy blocked much of the sun's light. "You'll tell us, though, right? If any ghosts show up?"

With a confirming nod, Emma took the lead, and Leo fell back alongside Mia. Each of them kept their head on a swivel.

He wanted to help Emma as best he could, but this was nuts. No matter how careful they were, how could they be expected to guard themselves against a witch? Especially if Monique—and Emma, by extension—led them straight into a trap.

"Emma, are you sure we should trust what Monique told us? What if this road leads us into a swamp?"

"She said I'd know where I was going." Emma stepped confidently forward. "And I do. I'm seeing ghosts now. Some are walking along with us, and some are just standing there, but they're all facing toward the woods."

Leo looked around, as if he'd be able to see the ghosts too. "They're not attacking you?" He couldn't help thinking of the malevolent ghosts Emma had encountered in the Other, which she'd finally described to them that morning.

"No, none of these ghosts seem vicious. When Monique summoned me there to warn me a few days ago, she'd said to avoid eye contact, so that's what I'm doing." Emma's attention remained focused as she walked forward. "I'm not sure what to make of them. They're nodding at me."

Leo shivered, but he didn't allow his steps to falter. "That could be because we're walking into a trap they helped arrange. They'd approve of us following their breadcrumbs to our doom, wouldn't they? I'm looking for something to slot into the *Trust Monique* column here, but so far, it's not looking good."

"I hear you, but I've felt maliciousness from the Other, and I'm not getting that now. I think these ghosts are unrelated."

Leo pushed a branch to the side, holding it still for Mia to pass. "Like, unrelated to you or to Monique or Celeste?"

"None of the above. The ones I'm seeing now are all distinct, standing apart, like they aren't even aware of each other." Emma's voice went quieter, just loud enough to be heard as she walked on through the woods. "And I've never seen a ghost that's related to me. I've never seen my mother or my father."

Leo couldn't quite decipher the emotion in her voice.

"These ghosts are from different eras. Some are dressed from centuries ago. Some could've stepped off a New York street yesterday."

"Let's face it. Anyone in elaborate historical dress could've stepped off the streets of New York City yesterday." Mia caught up to Emma.

Leo watched as the two women moved in tandem. Their recent trip through a dense woodland remained fresh in his mind, and he, again, found himself scanning the ground for trip wires and disturbed earth that might indicate a pit or other trap.

Emma described the ghosts she was seeing, and he figured she was doing it to kill the tension while giving them some insight into the Other. He wished it helped, but his nerves were strung as tight as a bowstring, as Papu, his grandfather, might've said.

Emma paused at a tree, scrolling on her phone. "It should

be a quarter mile ahead. Monique should've mentioned she had a long driveway."

"Ugh. This is next-level." Mia stopped to stretch her calf.

"Glad we got all that practice hiking on the last case." Leo winked at her.

Twisting her mouth into a wry smile, Emma gestured for them to follow. Mia went ahead.

Leo moved to join them, but before he took a step, the world tilted, throwing him completely out of touch with his surroundings.

Shadows shifted around him. There were beech and birch trees, but figures crowded between them, much like Emma described. He couldn't tell if they were people or ghosts or his imagination. Emma and Mia were still up ahead, but it looked like the color had been leached out of them.

What the hell is happening?

Mia glanced back at him and waved for him to catch up. "Leo? You okay back there?"

"I…" He closed his eyes and shook his head. Upon opening them again, his vision cleared. The sense of being in a shadowy version of this world dissipated. As he hurried to catch up to them, his equilibrium returned. "It's like my mind fuzzed out for a second. I don't know. Must've been my imagination or something. It didn't feel natural, it was so sudden."

There's one for the Don't Trust Monique *column, if that's a category.*

Emma stepped closer, up beside Mia, and frowned. "Is it gone now? Are you cold?"

He shook his head. "No, not cold. My vision got… shadowy. Like there was something gauzy in front of my face. Are either of you feeling odd?"

Emma frowned. "I'm fine. Mia?"

Mia shook her head. "Trust me, if I felt anything like that, I'd speak up right away."

Emma glanced around at what Leo had to imagine were ghosts. "Maybe Celeste was right, and Monique means us harm. But I think we have to keep going. She's had plenty of time to put together a welcoming committee, and we've made it this far."

He rubbed his temples, even though everything seemed to be in working order again. "But her first target would be Celeste, right? She wouldn't attack us yet, because we haven't brought Celeste with us."

Mia met Leo's gaze and nodded. "There's not really anything else we can do but move forward, right?"

Except run home with our tails between our legs.

Leo gestured Emma forward, even though he felt anything but reassured.

His mind remained steady as Emma went back to describing the ghosts around them. Finally, as they rounded a turn, she came to an abrupt stop, pointing at a small structure just ahead.

5

Emma had somehow imagined a dark, decrepit cabin, something like the shack they'd discovered on their last case. But Monique's cabin was alive with energy and appeared to be well-kept. The only thing run-down about it was a rusted dark-green Ford truck standing on bald tires at the end of the dirt track.

In the corner of the yard, an herb garden was neatly tended, and a stack of firewood sat to one side of the cabin beneath a lean-to structure. Just beyond the garden crouched a small greenhouse.

Emma stepped closer to the house, nearly expecting some birds to flit out of the woods and announce their presence or start singing a song about a princess.

The front porch held a rocking chair beside a short table. Three white candles and an old romance novel sat there. Ferns hung from above. The door was painted a welcoming green that blended in with the foliage.

"Monique Varley?" Hesitant to go closer, Emma called from the yard. "Monique, it's Emma. Are you here?"

The door opened seconds later, and the other woman in

the photograph with Emma's mother hurried onto the porch. She looked just as she had when she'd visited Emma in the Other.

Monique had not aged as gracefully as Celeste, but she was still handsome. Long grayish-brown hair hung free around her face, framing her rosy cheeks and ice-blue eyes. Wearing worn jeans and an old Foreigner t-shirt with sneakers, she looked as if she could be stepping outside for a stroll. A bright, toothy grin dominated her face.

"Emma, I'm so glad…" She broke off, faltering. "Are you okay?"

"Hi, Monique. Yes. I'm perfectly fine." Emma tried to appear casual, as Monique had clearly already read something different in her face. "And these are my colleagues, Special Agents Mia Logan and Leo Ambrose."

The smile slipped several degrees. "Very formal, I see."

Emma stepped forward. "Would it be all right if we sat down together? We're hoping you can help us understand what's been happening in Salem lately."

Any remnant of Monique's previous grin vanished. The woman stopped five feet away from Emma, glancing back and forth between the three of them, her icy eyes calculating. Finally, she nodded, as if in agreement with herself. "Celeste found you."

Emma sucked in her breath. She'd planned on saying as little as possible but changed her mind. "Detective Foss also told us she was the one who cast the protective spell on me. Just like you said you had. So, as you can imagine, I'm keeping an open mind."

Monique didn't seem surprised. "Of course." Her lips pursed, but then her eyes widened. "You're FBI, so you can fingerprint things, right? With some tool you carry around in your car?"

Leo stepped up beside her. "It's not quite that simple, Dr. Varley."

Emma held her gaze, wondering what on earth Monique was thinking. "We can run fingerprints if we need to, but we didn't come in a Bureau vehicle or bring any kit with us. Even if we had, how will that tell us we can trust you?"

Monique turned on her heel with a wave, speaking over her shoulder. "I still have the note your mother wrote me when I cast the protection spell. Give me a second. Grab a seat. Only my fingerprints and your mother's will be on it."

The woman disappeared inside, and Mia leaned closer. "That would be almost thirty years ago, but if she kept the note protected, we could possibly lift a print from the page."

"But fingerprints degrade based on any number of factors. So if she didn't protect it..." A surge of hope lifted Emma's spirits. "If it's in ink or blood or something, we could definitely use it. The handwriting might help too. We have analysts at the Bureau. I can find a known sample of Mom's handwriting, I'm pretty sure."

"You don't need to be a witch to forge things." Leo's harsh whisper faded as Monique hurried back out the door.

She pulled a page from the envelope in her hand. "I have it here."

Emma shifted closer as Monique read the letter aloud.

"'Monique, Emma and I are forever in your debt for this spell. I know what resources it cost you and what peace of mind. I can only hope it's not necessary, and that we'll all look back on this day and laugh, but I fear Celeste's rage can't be taken for granted. Who'd ever have thought she'd make such storms over a childhood pact? And so, again, I just have to say thank you. If my worst fears should come true, I hope you will stay safe, and that, one day, you'll be able to share this letter with Emma. I love you both with all my heart.'"

Emma's emotions blocked her throat, and she struggled

to hold her shit together. She'd seen that exact handwriting before and knew it well.

Still…

Monique passed the letter over, but Emma held her hands clear. "That could be evidence, and I don't want to contaminate it. Do you have a plastic bag?"

Shaking her head, the older woman held up the envelope. "Will this suffice? Only my and Gina's fingerprints will be on the letter. Please." Her gaze roved over Leo and Mia, even as Emma took the envelope. "She couldn't leave Emma a note directly. It would've put her husband and Emma in danger."

Emma studied her mother's large, loopy letters, spelling Monique's name across the front of the envelope. She balanced it gingerly on her palms, as though it were made of fragile glass.

This is your mom's handwriting, Emma girl. Complete with the little line marking the top of the i *instead of a dot. Dad always complained about that when he was teaching you cursive. Didn't want you to have "Mom's scrawl."*

Trying to remain neutral and focused, Emma met Monique's eyes. "Can you tell us your side of the story?"

Monique gestured for them to follow her inside. "I'll get us all some water. Unopened bottles. Don't want you worried about poison or anything."

Emma pocketed the envelope, and the three of them moved deeper into the cabin. Its cozy interior matched what she'd expected based on the serene, almost idyllic, exterior.

Two overstuffed armchairs sat across from a daybed, framing a sitting area around a hearth where herbs hung. The mantel held photographs in frames and vases of trimmed flowers and greenery.

Handmade drawings of plants and wildlife decorated the walls, and the open space boasted a small, neat kitchen on one side. One other door, beside the kitchen, led to a bathroom. A closed door across the way most likely marked the bedroom.

Monique came back with cold water bottles and passed them out. Emma only looked down at hers long enough to make sure the cap was indeed sealed before twisting it open and taking a deep gulp of the cool water.

She took a seat in one of the armchairs, and Leo and Mia sat together on the daybed. Monique took the other armchair, angling herself to face Emma.

"Your mother and Celeste and I grew up together. We were more like siblings." She paused, glancing between the three of them. "Perhaps like the three of you seem to be now. I sense a strong bond of trust."

Emma lowered the water bottle to her lap. "My mom trusted you and Celeste. At least, that's what you both want me to believe. I'm still not sure I do."

Monique nodded. "I understand. Gina did trust us both. At first, we were inseparable, the three of us."

Her eyes glazed over. Emma leaned forward, desperate to get closer to the source of her mother's history.

Wiping away a tear, Monique cleared her throat. "Let me start at the real beginning. I can't remember quite how it started, but I can tell you that it began at the clearing. This was back in the days when parents didn't care where you wandered or how far you went. Celeste always wanted to go farther and farther. She didn't have the greatest childhood."

If Monique's sympathy for her former friend was faked, she did a good job of it.

"The clearing?" Emma rolled her water bottle between her palms, glad for something to do with her hands.

"Yes. There's a clearing in the forest near here, almost a perfect circle. We called it the Place of Moonlight. We'd been hiking through the preserve and wandered into the circle without realizing we'd done so, until we all saw them."

Emma swallowed. "Them?"

"Shades. They had white eyes. They spoke in riddles. Gina and I were uncomfortable at first, but even on that first day, Celeste, without any hesitation, sat to speak with them."

"What was she doing?"

Monique twisted her fingers together. "Communing? Questioning? She always told us she was doing them a favor, lending a sympathetic ear to spirits who felt abandoned by the world, trapped and unable to progress fully into death."

I knew Monique could see ghosts—Shades—and move in the Other. Seems that Celeste can do the same.

"How often did you visit the clearing? The Place of Moonlight?"

Monique smiled. "Ever the investigator. A lot. The three of us went there often when we were younger. I think from the ages of eleven to fifteen, we were there at least once a week, sometimes for hours at a time. The more time we spent in the clearing, the more strange things we noticed afterward."

"What strange things?" Mia scooted to the edge of the daybed, like a kid listening to a ghost story.

Which is kind of what we're doing.

"It was like the space would infuse us. I started being able to sense the emotions of animals, something I can still do. Gina could stir cups of hot chocolate, even prepare a full meal, all without touching a single utensil. Celeste was always able to find things simply by asking the Shades. She didn't even have to be near the Place of Moonlight."

Mia raised one hand, just slightly, to pause her. "We're talking about superpowers?"

Monique wrinkled her nose. "You could describe things that way, I guess. For Gina and me, ours was a magic of life, of nurturing and protecting what we loved and who we loved. I cared for the animals I encountered. Still do in my work as a veterinarian. Gina prepared so many grand feasts, single-handedly. Birthdays, graduations, you name it."

"What about Celeste?"

Monique shifted in her chair, as if prodded by a knife. "She…at first, she used her powers to help others. At some point, she decided that 'finding' could also mean 'delivering.' She somehow figured out how to command the Shades to help her locate objects. Then she tried to use the same influence she had with the spirits on the living. Gina and I tried to convince her she was doing more harm than good. For a while, it seemed we'd succeeded. But Celeste kept practicing in secret, away from Gina and me."

Emma sipped from her water. "What happened between you? Why couldn't you and Mom stop her?"

Monique sat back in her chair, folding her arms. "We weren't willing to cross the same line she was. And then, when Gina met, and later married, Charles Last, that was the end. Celeste was furious."

"Why?"

"When we were thirteen, we made a pact in the Place of Moonlight. Celeste considered the space truly sacred and anything we did there to be sacrosanct."

Emma narrowed her eyes. "What was the pact you made with Mom and Celeste? What was it for?"

"We made a silly blood oath, as teenagers, mind you, to remain single." Monique closed her eyes for a brief moment. "The three of us would be together for life, as a family. No marriage meant our family would stay intact."

"A blood oath?" Emma didn't like the sound of that.

"We cut our palms and pressed them together. It's nothing fancy. But the Place of Moonlight gave it some power. I suppose we all felt the conviction of our promise at the time. None of us were the type to be planning our weddings and dreaming of Prince Charmings. By the time we reached adulthood, Gina and I basically forgot about the oath."

"But not Celeste."

"Not Celeste." Monique's expression darkened. "That oath became a road map for her. She planned her whole life around it and insisted the pact was unbreakable. Gina's… rejection stung like a poisoned barb to her heart."

Leo leaned forward. "What happened?"

"After Gina and Charles got engaged, Celeste began raving about the pact. She tried convincing Gina to call off the marriage. Celeste viewed Gina's marriage to Charles as a violation, as if exchanging vows with your father meant Gina was abandoning her family." Monique sighed, her shoulder slumping. "I tried to explain how ridiculous that was to Celeste when her behavior became too aggressive."

Leo jerked his chin at Emma. "And if your mother was half as stubborn as you, I doubt she'd have taken Celeste's temper tantrum lying down."

Monique snorted. "Right. Gina just cut off contact with us both."

"She didn't trust either of you?" Emma wasn't entirely sure who to trust either. Monique's story sounded honest, but she could be an accomplished liar. She'd had years to develop this tale, after all.

A sad frown made Monique appear years older. "For the first few months after the wedding, we both thought Gina had abandoned us for good. While I understood her need to protect herself, I'll never forget those lonely months. It brought me back to a time in my childhood before we'd all met each other. I used to be painfully shy, spend all my time alone, climbing trees and catching butterflies, sure, but alone."

Mia stood and walked over to the mantel, where a framed

photograph rested beside a bunch of fresh herbs and flowers in a vase. "This is the three of you."

"Yes. I believe you also have a copy of that picture, don't you, Emma?"

Emma joined Mia and examined the image. It was a duplicate of the one she'd been carrying around for the last few weeks.

"I've spent so much time staring at that photo, looking for some clue about my mother, or why she died." Emma nodded at the photo. "Doesn't look like you stayed estranged, though. I know you and Mom were friends until she died. What about Celeste?"

Monique wiped at tears brimming in her eyes. "You're right. One day, Gina just showed up, explaining how much she missed us. She wanted to mend the bridges. Celeste's mood shifted. She welcomed Gina, and everything returned to a semblance of before."

"What happened to wreck that?" Emma was pretty sure she wouldn't like the answer.

"You." Monique took a sip of her water. "On the night Gina shared her pregnancy news with us, she and I were forced to accept Celeste's true nature. Or, rather, what her nature had become."

"What about her nature?"

Monique shuddered with emotion. "I'm afraid Celeste is responsible for your mother's death. She considered that oath we took as binding, a pact none of us would dare break."

Emma handed the photo to Mia, though she didn't take her focus off Monique. She squared her shoulders. "That is a grievous charge." It could also be a ploy to convince Emma that Monique wasn't responsible for the violent events taking over Salem, but she kept that doubt to herself.

"Celeste declared that no child would ever leave Gina's

womb alive. She claimed to have laid a curse on your mother. In her twisted mind, she thought that with the baby dead, your parents' relationship would crumble, and Gina would rejoin us."

"Why would Celeste want that? So the three of you could keep playing witch games in the woods?" Emma waved away Monique's surprised expression at her bluntness. "Sorry, this is a lot to hear, and...forgive me...that motive sounds like bullshit."

"What you must understand is that Celeste was incredibly lonely as a child, and we were her closest family. Her parents died when she was young. She was raised by a great-aunt who loved her garden more than Celeste. She's always felt abandoned and lonely." Monique squinted at Emma. "Maybe you can relate a little?"

The question was so direct, it took Emma's breath away. Yes, she'd been lonely as a child. Her father was always busy. She'd gone to boarding schools.

Monique seemed to sense that her question had hit its mark. "Celeste was hoping that when Gina came around, she'd get serious about the sisterhood again and we'd be what we once were. A trio of young women, devoted to one another and to no one else. She never understood how Gina just walked away from us, from her power, in college."

"Mom walked away from her power?"

Monique gestured around her. "Celeste and I never abandoned our connection to the Other. But your mother? She dropped it entirely once she met Charles. She considered our antics a part of her girlhood, childish things to be put away. 'Her wild and supernatural years,' she called them. I think that was the beginning of Celeste's commitment to the magic of manipulation and control."

"So what?" Leo grimaced, watching Monique with a suspicious expression. "I mean, most of the people we meet in high school and college disappear from our lives, never to return. We go our separate ways and maybe see each other at the twenty-year reunion."

"That isn't how Celeste operates. Her childhood was empty. She wants family but doesn't understand how family actually works. A lone wolf, if you will. Now add that to the fact that we'd discovered another world, the Other, and we could see its inhabitants." Monique pressed her palms together. "Now pile on superpowers, as Mia called them, and we were bonded beyond blood. The kind of connection no one thought would be broken. It's a very unique secret that you can't actually share with anyone."

It certainly was the kind of secret that was hard to share. Emma knew that firsthand.

Monique sighed. "I do understand why Celeste was devastated when Gina got pregnant. She'd left us once and returned to just break our hearts again. Think about that. Celeste thought she was back for good. Thought she'd start practicing again to regain her powers. Thought we'd be unstoppable." She shrugged. "But I also understand Gina's motivation too. She fell in love. And sure, she missed her best friends. But ultimately, romantic love won, and she wanted to start a family."

"So my mom and dad falling in love broke Celeste's heart the first time around, but then my mom wanting a child devastated her beyond repair?" Emma dropped back into the armchair, her gaze still fixed on Monique.

"Like getting dumped by the love of your life, twice." Mia shook her head, also resuming her seat on the daybed.

"Yes, that's a good way of putting it."

"And then she cast some curse to destroy Gina's baby?" Leo spoke more confidently, but his earlier cynicism still bit into his tone. "But Emma's here, so it couldn't have worked."

Monique searched Emma's face, and a deep, foreboding groan escaped the woman's lips. "Oh, trust me, the curse worked. Just not as Celeste intended."

6

Emma wavered where she sat, struggling to remain centered. Her neutrality was failing her. She sensed a ring of truth in Monique's story, but was she merely chasing the easiest, most available truth? Monique was giving her a reason for her mother's slow and painful death beyond being unlucky and dying young of cancer. And she was also offering up a villain.

Beside her, Leo muttered something under his breath, and Mia shushed him, but the room was heavy with tension that couldn't be ignored.

Monique locked eyes with Emma. "Your mother made a choice. For both of you."

A choice.

The words echoed in Emma's mind, and she wasn't sure she wanted to know, but she asked anyway. "What was it?"

"She came to me for help." Monique raised her face to the ceiling and closed her eyes. The water bottle fell onto the seat of the armchair beside her as tears dripped down her cheeks, sudden and clear. "I searched and searched for any option that could help you and her both. Gina was desperate.

I found a way to transfer Celeste's curse to a different target, but doing so required physical contact. We had only one available target to step in for an unborn child."

Emma's throat closed, emotion blocking it as her heart pounded.

A choice.

"You transferred whatever it was," she couldn't bring herself to say the word *curse*, "from me to Mom."

Mia hopped up from the daybed and wrapped her arms around Emma.

"You mustn't blame yourself." Monique's tone was soft and comforting, but Emma didn't feel comforted.

"I don't." Emma's tone was flat. "I'm not the one who made the *whatever*, and I'm not the one who transferred the *whatever* to Mom."

Monique held out her hands. "Please, you have to understand. I was like a sister to Gina. I didn't want to hurt her. But she wanted you to live. That's all. It had to be done."

Emma couldn't bring herself to look at Monique. She examined the weave of the rug beneath her feet. Whatever she'd been prepared for, it hadn't been the news that Gina Last had traded her own life for that of her daughter.

Her mom's friend leaned forward and gripped Emma's hand where it clung to the chair arm. "I helped her. I took on a protective spell for you."

Emma jerked her hand away. She gulped from her water bottle, looking at the floor, again letting Monique talk, even though the words hit her like barbs.

"It was all I could do. Gina grew ill, but you remained healthy. She stayed hidden at home so Celeste wouldn't discover what we'd done. According to Gina's doctor, you were thriving. Celeste assumed the opposite."

"How did you keep me hidden, though? I was born. I didn't die. Celeste had to know her thing didn't work."

"When the illness progressed to the point that her doctor began fearing for your life, she and Charles hired a live-in nurse who was also a midwife. We thought everything would be fine, and your birth went smoothly. Charles, of course, announced the news at his law firm. Someone told someone else, and Celeste learned of your birth."

"And Mom was still okay." Emma's voice was a soft, fragile thing, but she pictured her mother in that photograph she kept by the side of her bed. The one that fell down all the time. The joy on Gina Last's face. Her survival *was* what her mother had wanted. She had to remember that. "I lived, and so did she."

"For a while." Monique nodded sadly. "Then Celeste found out what we'd done."

Mia gripped Emma's shoulders, and Emma leaned into her. It was so easy to see now how the women's friendship had disintegrated and the terrible sacrifice her mother had been forced to make.

Monique shifted in her seat, raking one sleeve against her cheeks to dry them. "I tried to forget all that had happened, if you want the truth. Losing Gina was so painful. I thought you were well protected and would be out of Celeste's view if I was out of the picture."

Losing Gina was so painful. The understatement of the century.

She looked around the room, focusing on details Emma could only guess at. "After that, I established the wards that keep her at bay and to protect myself." She pointed to a spray of herbs hanging by the door, then to a second display by the window, and a third in the kitchen. "I have them in every room, at every possible point of entry. I also keep them hanging throughout the preserve."

Emma jerked her head up. "Why do you live so close to the Place of Moonlight, while Celeste lives in the city? It seems like she held this place more sacred than you or my mother did."

Monique sucked in a deep breath. "The reason for my presence here, so close to the clearing that became Celeste's focus, is simple. As long as I live, my protective ward will ensure your safety. I can only keep that promise if I remain tethered to the Place of Moonlight."

Emma gnawed her lip. "Even after all this time, you've stayed out here alone because you didn't want to risk Celeste's rage being directed your way?"

"Yes. If she kills me, you'll be vulnerable to her attacks. The gate prevents Celeste from coming in here. But I can't keep her out of the Place of Moonlight. We found that clearing together. It's on the preserve, so it's public property."

The gate? That rusty green thing we walked around?

"But something changed."

Monique sat back in the chair as her gaze danced over them. "Your mother died at twenty-eight, as you know. And as your twenty-eighth birthday neared, as I'd suspected, you came into your full power, which allowed you to see into the Other and interact with it. This also made you fully visible to the Other and to those of us who are also able to interact with that realm."

"Like you and Celeste." Monique's story made sense with Emma's experience. But that didn't mean she wasn't lying about her part in it all.

They both might be telling the truth, or they both might be lying. The real threat may be from the Other itself, for all you know.

Emma couldn't help thinking that Monique didn't look much like a witch right now in that ratty Foreigner t-shirt. But she supposed supernatural people, like criminals, could look like anyone. After all, she had successfully hidden her own abilities while working for the FBI.

"Celeste said she wanted the three of us to work together against you. She said you were responsible for the crime wave happening in Salem."

Monique nodded sadly. "If you take her up on that, that will be the beginning of the end for me and you. To break my protective ward over you, she has to kill me. Then she'll be free to kill you. And my promise to Gina will have been for nothing."

Emma searched for words but had none. Her whole body was frozen with the intake of history and information.

Seeming to sense Emma's struggle, Monique stood. "You all need time and space to talk. Emma, you need to process without one of your mother's old friends staring at you. I'm emotionally exhausted, so I know you must be as well."

Shoving herself to her feet, Emma looked at Leo and Mia. "Time we got moving, yeah?"

They both stood, with Leo making a beeline to the door.

Monique held out her arms. "May I give you a hug, Emma? Please?"

Emma shrank back. "I don't think that'd be appropriate, especially with your ability to feel emotions. We are all animals, after all."

"Well, that's all right, then." Monique dropped her arms to her side and stood awkwardly looking at the three of them. "We got it all out into the air. Cell phones don't work out here, but all of you, please, come back when you're ready. We'll figure this out, and I'll help however I can."

Somewhat dazed, Emma offered a smile in response before following her friends outside. The front door closed softly behind them.

When they reached the woods at the edge of Monique's firebreak, Mia ran her hands through her hair. "Do you trust her?"

Yes. Maybe. No.

"I'm not sure." Emma picked her way forward along the road through the woods, leading the way back to the car. "They both feel very straightforward. One of them is a very good criminal, using the motivation of the other one as her own. There's a lot riding on this. And the letter doesn't prove much. I don't have my mother's fingerprints on record anywhere, so we can't check, even if we had a fancy fingerprint doodad in our car."

"Maybe we can find a handwriting sample at that family home you mentioned?" Mia nodded at the envelope in Emma's pocket.

"Yeah, maybe, but it's been a while since I've been to the house. I don't know what's there. DNA is unlikely or trustworthy, given we have no way to confirm chain of custody either. We have nothing to verify her story."

Mia almost tripped but caught herself on a tree. "I know we're not here officially, but Celeste asked for our help earlier when she hunted you down at the hotel. We could just do what we do."

"Investigate?" Leo gave her half a smile.

"We can watch Celeste and still do some good. She's working a lot of cases right now. There's the neighbor who strangled the old lady whose lawn he used to mow. Damien Knight."

"You're right." Emma walked faster, trying to ignore the various ghosts—Shades—nodding at her as she moved. She wished she'd thought to ask Monique how to block them out. "There's been a crime wave, and Salem's cops are probably overwhelmed. Let's start there. We'll keep Celeste as close as we can without giving her too much information. We'll watch her."

Emma gave in to Leo's insistence that he take the wheel once they got back to the Malibu. She really wanted to drive.

It was like an itch in her body. But he didn't relinquish the key fob, insisting she could still "wig out" on them.

Once they were all belted in and Leo had started the engine, her mind turned to more immediate matters. "I'm starving. Who else is ready to sample the local fare before we talk to Salem's finest?"

7

They grabbed a quick lunch at a diner, focusing more on the food than conversation, and were back on the road by two thirty. Emma listened to Leo as he pointed out landmarks, like the historic House of Seven Gables. Whatever had happened to him in the woods, it seemed to have eased.

Just keep an eye on your friend, Emma girl.

"Would not live there. Not for a million dollars. Two million maybe, but…nope. Not even that much would get me to sleep in that house."

Mia laughed from the back seat, and Emma joined in. Leo must've been hangry earlier. He was all smiles and good humor now.

Even as she put that worry out of her mind, Emma's stomach clenched with tension around Salem's crime wave. She got her phone out and scrolled through crime reports from recent weeks. The details became stranger and stranger the more crimes she unearthed.

Fights between longtime friends with no history of animosity. In those cases, the charges were almost always dropped, except in one wherein the fight had led to someone being beaten so badly, they ended up in the hospital.

The assailant in that case was charged with battery by the D.A., but his victim refused to press any charges of their own. Maybe they'd get some answers after speaking with the arresting officers.

Leo pulled up to the station and parked behind two cruisers on the curb. He glanced over at Emma before undoing his seat belt. "Any more attacks of cold?"

"Nothing since before we visited Monique." Emma opened the door, shrugging the rest of the way into her FBI jacket as she climbed out. "Comparatively speaking, I don't know if that's good news at this point."

In the lobby, the desk attendant spoke into her phone while eyeing their jackets and badges. "Officer in charge here'll be right with you folks. Take a seat."

By the time they got to the row of chairs lining the side of the lobby, the desk officer had apparently changed her mind and come out from behind the counter. Young and blond, she peered between them before focusing in on Mia. "You're out of D.C., right? You all were involved in cutting off a gang war? Detective Foss told me about it. I knew you looked familiar."

Mia's cheeks warmed, but she nodded. "We were. I ended up doing a lot of the press."

The woman dug into her pocket and pulled out a card, suddenly awkward. She pressed it forward into Mia's hand. "I'm Officer Sandra Vales. I'm on the front desk here more often than not. Some people think I'm not as scary as the rest of our force, but that's because they haven't seen me at my best." She winked. "If you all need anything while you're in town, just ask."

Thanking her, Mia tucked the card away, and Emma rested back in her seat. Vales returned to her desk as a short, mustached cop came out the side door with a confused frown. "Officer Michael Konig at your service. Can I help you? We didn't hear anything about a visit from the Feds today."

Emma stood and held out her hand. "I'm Special Agent Emma Last. These are my colleagues, Special Agents Leo Ambrose and Mia Logan. Detective Celeste Foss invited us to look into a few cases, and we were hoping to hear the details of the attack involving Damien Knight last night. Maybe you could help us?"

The officer's lips pursed. "I was the arresting officer for that case. You here to tell me what I did wrong?"

Emma didn't take his attitude personally. No one enjoyed having their cases reviewed. "Absolutely not."

"Foss called you all in?" As he squinted at them each in turn, Emma got a distinct Popeye vibe.

She offered her most unassuming smile, hoping they wouldn't have to get Jacinda involved. "Yes, sir. Just this morning. We're just trying to collect information."

Konig frowned but led them back through the side door and into an empty bullpen. He waved for them to follow him to a break room. "Conference room is being renovated. Any of you want coffee?"

"We're fine. Just had some." Emma pulled out her tablet, taking a seat at the round table in the center of the room.

Mia and Leo settled into the chairs on either side of her.

When Konig sat down opposite them, she prodded him. "So the Pheobe Wilson case…"

"I don't know how the Wilson case got on your radar. Or maybe I do. Probably the craziest thing I've seen in a year. You've seen the news around town, I'm guessing?" They nodded, and he gave a sad chuckle. "So you know what I mean when I say 'crazy.'"

Emma brought up a headline showing Damien Knight's

name and spun the tablet so Konig could read it. "We know this matches with a lot of news around Salem lately. People behaving erratically, unexpected violence from otherwise peaceful and law-abiding neighbors."

"Right." He touched a finger to his mustache, smoothing it down. "It's baffling, is what it is. Knight's got no criminal history. Man grew up here. Nobody can figure it. But we caught his arrival on Phoebe Wilson's home security system. He forces his way into the house, clear as day."

"And Phoebe Wilson...she was elderly." Leo waited, but the officer only nodded. "Any family?"

"Her husband, Albert, died a while back. They have a son. He joined the Navy and retired a few years ago and moved overseas to live with his spouse's family in the Philippines. We're getting word to him."

"What about enemies?"

The officer barked a laugh. "Did Phoebe Wilson have enemies? She could ruffle feathers all day, but I wouldn't say she earned the kind of attention that leads to murder."

"Whose feathers did she ruffle?" Emma motioned for him to continue.

Konig tapped a pen on his chin. "I remember her causing an uproar at a city hall meeting a few years ago. Something about the city's animal shelter going from no-kill to... whatever the other kind is."

"They were talking about euthanizing animals, and she got upset." Mia clasped her hands on the table in front of her. "Anything come of it?"

"Hell yes." The officer shrugged. "She put on her old-lady teaching voice, and that was that. Shelter's still no-kill and proud of it. I'm sure she had some students who didn't like her back in her day, but she's been retired for twenty years."

Closing her tablet cover, having barely taken any notes,

Emma decided to press their luck. "Do you think we could talk to Knight? Just briefly?"

The man shifted his gaze among them. "I don't know what you'll get out of him, but I guess you're welcome to try. He just keeps repeating the same thing. Get Foss to sign off, though, and I'll let you have a go."

"Can you call her down?"

"I'll go get her." Konig left the break room.

Once the door swung closed behind him, the trio turned toward one another.

"If you're so convinced Celeste is behind all the mayhem, do you think it's a good idea to let her know we're taking a crack at one of her perpetrators?" Leo glanced at the closed door, as if nervous of being overheard.

Emma shook her head. "Keep your friends close—"

"—and your enemies closer," Mia finished. "Works for me. But if what Monique said is true, Celeste is very dangerous to have close by."

"She might be more dangerous to have at a distance."

The door swung open again, and in stalked Celeste Foss. Emma wondered if she'd been watching them in the security cameras, or if she'd established a ghost patrol in the Other to keep tabs on Emma's whereabouts.

Konig entered right behind her.

Celeste, for her part, looked a bit relieved to see them. Her dark eyes were brighter than earlier this morning. A small smile even turned her otherwise tight, professional lips upward. "Agents. I'm glad you've come in to help. We need it. I hear you want to talk to Damien Knight. What do you think, Konig?"

For a moment, Emma thought Konig would disagree, but he sighed and straightened up, waving at Emma to follow him. "I don't see how one of you talking to him could hurt. Not all three. Don't want to overwhelm him.

But the man's so torn up, he'd probably like someone to talk to."

"Then let's show you where he is." Celeste opened the door and waved for everyone to follow her.

Emma kept to Konig's heels. "You say he's torn up? Upset?"

"Like somebody killed his own mother. Like he's a victim rather than the killer that did the strangling." Konig led her through a cramped office to a row of three cells beyond. In the middle one, a large redheaded man sat on the cot with his head in his hands. They all paused just outside the entryway.

"I'll take it from here." Celeste dismissed Konig with a tight nod. Her professional, slightly cold demeanor had returned. Once Konig was away, however, she turned to Emma's team. "He can't remember what he's done. I think Monique has managed to do some kind of mind control. She used to be able to do it with animals. I think she might be escalating and turning people into her puppets."

Emma remembered Monique was a veterinarian who could empathize with animals, not control them. *All good lies have an element of truth.*

"Thank you, Detective Foss." Emma straightened her shoulders. "Though I appreciate your input, if you want our help, we need to be able to draw our own conclusions. We'll approach this like a regular investigation."

Celeste shoved her hands deep inside her pockets. Emma wondered if it was an attempt to avoid slapping her across the face. She offered another of her neutral smiles. "I'll leave you to it, my girl." She turned to Mia and Leo. "I can get footage set up for you to review."

"Sounds good." Leo lifted an eyebrow at Emma as a silent question to see if she was okay.

Emma nodded.

"My shift is over. Been working doubles. But if you need

me, just stop by my house." Celeste pulled out her notebook, scrawled her address across the page, and handed it to Emma. "Give Konig a holler when you're done here."

Celeste turned on a heel and walked out, with Leo and Mia following closely behind to review security footage from Phoebe Wilson's murder.

Emma smiled at her as the woman retreated, leaving her to face Damien Knight in his cell. "Mr. Knight?"

He remained hunched over, hands on his ears. When she repeated his name, and he finally looked up, his eyes were red. He swiped at them with a giant hand. "I'm him."

His voice was soft, wispy, as if he'd been choked himself. And his red-rimmed eyes spoke of hours spent sobbing.

"Mr. Knight, I'm Special Agent Emma Last, with the FBI. I'm hoping you can help me understand what happened last night. Could you do that?"

He swallowed, then leaned back against the cement wall behind the cot. Licking his lips, he took a few long seconds to consider his answer before speaking. "I don't really know. Phoebe was family to me, but they say I killed her." He choked off a sob, pulling one hand through his beard and landing it over his chest before he spoke again. "They *showed* me video, from her camera. They said I 'forced my way in' and killed her. But I don't remember doing it."

"What do you remember?"

"I was watching television." His brows knitted together. "A game had just started. I was thinking about giving my sister a call but thought it might be too late and I'd wake my nieces."

The man looked like he might break into sobs again, so Emma bent in front of the bars to catch his gaze. "You said you were watching a game. Who was playing?"

He shook his head. "Doesn't matter, does it? Phoebe's

dead. They say I did it, but how can that be true? It can't be true. I don't remember. I wouldn't hurt her."

"You knew Phoebe well. You had a friendship with her?"

Knight wrenched himself back and forth on his cot. He settled down and wiped his eyes. "I mowed her lawn. Helped her carry in groceries. She was too old to be living on her own but wouldn't hear of anything else."

"You suggested she move in with someone or move to a retirement home?"

He nodded. "We were always friendly. I don't know why I'd do that."

Emma opened her mouth to say something, but tears were drifting down the man's face again. He bent over his knees, head in hands, and she simply stepped away. She looked back toward the entrance and saw Konig had been waiting for her on the opposite side of the space.

He waved her over.

"You get anything useful?" He spoke quietly, gaze on the man behind her. "Man's so broken up, I feel bad for him. Can't help it."

She nodded, matching his low volume. "Who turned him in?"

"Security company got an alert that the door was ajar. An address like that where the door doesn't even usually get opened after nine at night, they pulled up the footage to check right away. Thought Mrs. Wilson might've had an accident. And when they saw, they called 911. Arresting officers found him standing on the front porch like he was thinking about where to go next. He didn't put up a fight."

"Is that on the footage?"

"You bet. Your partners are already viewing it." He led the way back to the bullpen, where Mia and Leo were seated in front of a laptop.

Leo gave her a small nod. Emma moved around to his

shoulder, and he took the slider bar back to begin replaying the footage.

Damien Knight stood on a small front porch, swaying. His lips were moving as if he were speaking, maybe muttering to himself.

Leo paused the playback. "Looks like he's intoxicated or drugged."

Or in a trance.

Emma would've been willing to bet he hadn't been party to his crime in anything but body. If she had to describe what she was seeing in Knight's behavior, she'd say his mind had been consumed by the Other.

Just like hers had been when Monique summoned her into the Other during their last case.

Leo shared a glance with her, clearly thinking the same, but neither of them could ask Konig to confirm their suspicions.

"Have you had time to get tox results in?"

"Yep, and the answer is no. That was our first thought, but he came up cleaner than an altar boy at Communion." Konig rubbed his chin. "Officers didn't find any alcohol or controlled substances in his house, either, not even prescription medications."

"What about outside his home? Did he go anywhere last night, before the attack?"

"He went to a pizza parlor around five thirty and didn't have anything harder than a soda."

Mia glanced up from the video. "You talked to the folks who served him?"

Konig nodded, frowning. "It's a mom-and-pop joint he's been going to since he was a kid. Owner said he was acting normal."

Emma sighed and looked up from the video. It was painful to connect the guilt- and grief-stricken bear of a man she'd just seen to the confused man in the video. "Have any other cases like this one been caught on camera?"

Konig shifted on his feet. "Yeah, a couple." He leaned over to click on the screen and pulled up another round of footage. "This was another weird one. Housewife by the name of Brittany Weir attacked a salesperson. I made this arrest too."

The footage from a Ring camera showed a man in pressed khakis and a polo shirt standing with his hand outstretched, handing a young woman a business card. She accepted it with a smile before going stock-still.

Seconds later, Brittany Weir's arms dropped to her sides, and her lips moved, as if she were muttering to herself like Damien Knight had done. The salesperson waved a hand in front of her face and backed up a step after that. He was either trying to take in the whole picture to gauge what was going on with her or just leaving when she launched at him.

By virtue of luck or fate, the salesperson was a far cry taller than Brittany, and she wasn't a gifted attacker. She grabbed him by his polo shirt and shoved him off the porch. He stumbled down the steps and landed hard on her grassy lawn. Brittany leaped down and directed a kick at the salesperson's legs. He rolled to the side and got to his feet. She followed him, kicking like crazy.

Before she could do any real damage, though, another body flew in front of the camera and began tugging her away from the man.

"Her husband, Trevor, pulled her off before she could really hurt the guy. Said he'd never seen her do anything like that. Both of 'em as confused as Knight in there."

The video ran, showing the husband's terrified face as he held his wife from behind, wrapping her in a bear hug and trapping her arms. He dragged her down to the ground so she couldn't kick the salesperson anymore.

Brittany eventually went limp in his arms and fell against his chest.

Konig cut the video. "We pulled a tox screen for her, same as with Knight. Nothing in her blood and no criminal history. Her husband begged us to search the house. He thought maybe she'd been taking something in secret. Didn't find anything. He's had everybody you can think of come out to that house since then. Checking for leaky chemicals, lead in the water, whatever. Anything that might've caused her to go berserk like that."

Emma filed away the information, but her mind burned with the voices of Celeste and Monique, each blaming the other for these events.

Without the supernatural in play, none of this made sense. And that meant that if Celeste Foss or Monique Varley were behind Salem's sudden crime wave, one of them had a much deeper and far more dangerous plan for the city.

8

Despite Leo annoying her behind the wheel again, Emma was at least free to search for information on Celeste Foss while he drove. She'd expected Celeste, like Monique, would keep her home address a secret. But the federal database Emma searched on her tablet spit out an address immediately.

Cross-referencing to a map of Salem, she sat back in the passenger seat. "She lives on the opposite side of the city from Monique, in the suburbs."

Mia leaned forward to get a glance at the information on Emma's tablet. "That street name looks familiar. I think Konig mentioned it."

Emma looked up the Weirs' address and hit paydirt. "Brittany and Trevor Weir live across the street from Celeste." She checked Phoebe Wilson's address next. "Phoebe Wilson and Damien Knight are one street over. Their backyard fences butt up against the Weirs' and their next-door neighbors'."

Leo whistled, keeping his eyes on the road. "That's a hell of a cluster, considering how large Salem is."

"So a cluster of some of the violent incidents are happening around Celeste's home. Do you think that's because Monique is trying to get to her?" Mia's eyebrows drew together.

"Who knows how this bullshit works." Emma didn't intend for her irritation to show. She should be the patient one—after all, *she* was the one who saw ghosts. "I can see either of them as the bad guy, using us to lead one to the other."

"So they can kill each other and maybe us in the process." Leo's tone held an undertone of irritation, just like her own.

She looked at Leo before turning to meet Mia's eyes.

Mia frowned. "What is it? Do I have something on my face or food in my teeth?"

A smile forced its way out of Emma, even as she feared for her friends' lives. "Just glad to have you both with me on this. I know I've thanked you before, but I'm grateful you're taking this risk, to be here with me."

Mia leaned forward. "We got you. We'll figure this out. Together."

They drove in silence for a while as Leo brought them closer to Celeste's neighborhood.

"How about we speak to her neighbors before we go straight to her?" Emma glanced at Leo, then Mia, gauging their reactions. "We have Monique's read on her but nobody else's. If we get more of the same from her neighbors, maybe we'll have something for the *Trust Monique* column."

Leo nodded, and Mia added her own agreement. "I'm in. If she *is* the epicenter of chaos, it's likely more than a few neighbors have noticed something."

"And if they haven't, we'll have more reason to consider Monique the threat." Leo flicked on his blinker and made a smooth turn.

Letting the conversation drop, Emma kept watch out her

window, doing her best to admire the city of her birth, even as its residents seemed hell-bent on tearing it apart.

Leo cruised into Celeste's neighborhood, driving by her unassuming Craftsman house and parking a block away. They got out, and Emma headed down the sidewalk to the corner house.

She knocked, and a voice hollered through an open window beside the door. "I got nothing to say to any FBI agents! Get lost!"

"Sir, we're not here to cause you any trouble. We're hoping you can help us with a case that's developing in the area."

"I said screw off. Unless you have a warrant, you're trespassing. Now get!"

Emma backed away from the door. "Let's go to the next house." She led the way one house over, and a middle-aged woman answered within a few seconds. Though Emma had gotten her hopes up, the glare she received was not welcoming.

"What do you Feds want?" A child's screech sounded from somewhere behind the woman, but she didn't so much as flinch. "Well? I got a kid needs his bath, and my show starts in twenty minutes."

"Ma'am, I'm Special Agent Last. With me are Special Agents Ambrose and Logan. We were hoping you could help us with a series of crimes affecting the area."

"This ain't about me personally? I ain't in trouble? Not that I should be."

Leo offered his most charming grin. "No, ma'am, absolutely not. We just—"

The door slammed in their faces.

They were batting a thousand.

"Maybe this neighborhood is just full of murderers, and we're making too much of this violent crime wave?" Emma sighed. "It could help if we take the jackets off. Blend in a little more, keep things low-key."

Leo shrugged by way of answer, then collected Mia's and Emma's jackets and walked them back to the Malibu. Now just in business casual, they headed to the next house, but Emma let Mia take the lead. Maybe her sweetness would get them somewhere.

An elderly Black man wearing slacks and suspenders answered the door. He smiled at her, then at Emma, and only squinted at Leo standing behind them.

"What can I do you folks for? Don't have much time. Got my dinner cookin' now."

Mia smiled bigger. "We won't take much of your time, sir. We're investigating the rash of violence that's been happening around Salem, quite a bit of it in this neighborhood. Would you be willing to talk to us about anything you've observed lately?"

He pursed his lips and hooked a thumb through a suspender. "Salem's gotten bad lately, it's true. My son works with the K-9 unit over at the department, and they're at a loss. They can use the help dealing with all the madness."

Emma nodded, hoping he'd get more specific before his dinner burned. "What sorts of madness have you observed?"

He ran a hand down his shirt. "The couple across the way and down some, the Weirs...they had something going on. I came outside because of the racket. Brittany's husband, Trevor, was screaming loud enough to scare the devil."

"Was that the first time you'd seen or heard them making a racket?"

The man nodded. "Two of them are more the type to organize neighborhood yard sales and walk around collecting canned goods for the food pantry. Never heard a peep from either of them until that day the salesman showed up. I don't know what he was selling, because he lit off out of the neighborhood after Brittany went at him like a wildcat."

Leo stepped a bit closer, one hand on the porch rail. "And was anything different about the neighborhood, leading up to that attack? New faces or unfamiliar cars driving through, anything like that?"

"Nah." He shook his head, gaze drifting down toward the Weirs' address. "It was a normal day, that's all I can tell you."

A timer went off from somewhere behind him, and he darted a glance over his shoulder. "If you don't mind, my dinner's calling."

"You've been more than helpful, sir. Thank you." Emma fought the urge to pull out a card to offer him. Instead, she simply nodded as he closed the door.

"Not much to go on, beyond more confirmation that the Weirs were normal."

Leo nodded. "I think we should try to talk to them before Celeste. Want to try another neighbor or two first?"

"Might as well." They walked back down the drive and up the next one to a little red cottage with neat black shutters. Leo rang the bell and stepped back so they could all view the door.

The brunette Caucasian woman who answered looked near their age, perhaps a few years younger, and carried an infant on her hip over a cream-colored apron printed with bounding jackrabbits and sunflowers. She smiled at them in a manner that seemed near enough like the last man, which seemed like a good start. "Can I help you all?"

"We're investigating the crimes that have occurred in this neighborhood, ma'am. Hoping you can help us understand what's been happening."

"You all cops? Feds? Look like Feds, but I don't see any badges."

Hoping it wouldn't mean another door being slammed in

their faces, Emma flashed her ID and badge. Leo nodded at Mia, and they did the same.

The woman eyed each of them in turn. "Feds. Just like I thought. I wondered when it'd get bad enough they'd call you all in."

Breathing a quick sigh of relief, Emma picked up the conversation. "The violence in Salem has been escalating. What can you tell us about recent events in your area?"

"You mean the business with Brittany." The woman's eyes sharpened, her gaze moving over their shoulders to the Weirs' house. "I swear, I don't know what happened. I know Brittany. I've even had her babysit Luca here a few times. This is Luca. I'm Mary Evert."

She jostled the baby, and Mia murmured how cute he was before going on. "So that must mean you trust her?"

"I did." Mary readjusted her baby as he cooed happily at her. "I wouldn't know, obviously. I was in the front room when the sales guy came around. I figured if he was over there, he'd be coming here soon enough, and I might as well be ready to tell him I didn't want any. I was watching out the window, so I could see if he came my way. When Brittany lost it, I went running outside."

"What did you see when you went outside?" Mia played with the baby's fingers but kept her focus on the mother.

Mary shook her head, smiling at her child's reaction to Mia's playing, but her face soon sagged with sorrow. "I saw Brittany shoving the salesman off the steps, and she started kicking at him."

That matched the video they'd seen, but Emma needed to know if Mary had noticed any details about the sudden shift in Brittany's behavior. "Did you notice anything unusual about her behavior before she shoved the salesperson off her porch?"

"Nothing I could put my finger on, but…something was off about her right before she started attacking the guy."

"Off?" Leo shifted his weight side to side.

Mary shrugged. "Like, she was a little slow and nervous, ya know? I have a nephew who does hard drugs, and in between fixes, he gets that faraway look, like he's not all there."

"Have you ever seen Brittany use hard drugs?"

"No!" Mary bounced the baby, but her jaw was tight. "She wouldn't. I'd know it if she did."

Emma homed in on the certainty in Mary's voice. "You and Brittany were close."

The woman's face fell. "We used to be, yeah. She's kept to herself since the attack."

She lowered her gaze. The baby began to whine but took Mia's finger again when it was offered.

"We'll let you go soon." Emma forced a smile for the baby's benefit as his eyes focused on her. "Have you noticed any of your other neighbors behaving unusually?"

"Other than the lady who lives across from Brittany and Trevor, you mean?" Mary's face twisted with disgust, and Emma had to fight the grin trying to curl across her lips.

"Who…what's the lady's name, who lives across from the Weirs?"

"Celeste. I think her last name is Faust, Officer Faust or something like that. I don't know her really, but she saw the attack too."

The way that Mary said Celeste's name made the back of Emma's neck prickle. "Okay, so you both saw what happened with Brittany. What else should we know?"

Mary shifted on her feet, jostling the baby on her hip.

"We're just exploring possibilities, ma'am." Leo gestured to his tablet. "Trying to find out whatever we can."

"Right. Of course." Mary sighed. "Well, like I said, I went

outside when Brittany attacked that man, and I saw movement in the officer's window. That woman, that Detective Faust, *smiled*. Not like a huge clown smile or anything. But she looked…satisfied. Smug, even. Struck me as strange. Why the heck wouldn't she run on out and protect and serve? Do her job?"

Emma kept her tone even, though in a weird way, this could be good news. "Did you mention Celeste's, Detective Foss's, behavior to anyone else?"

Adding one to the Trust Monique *column. Tentatively, but adding it just the same.*

Mary blushed, her cheeks going a bright pink. "I called 911 and talked to the responding officers, but I didn't think about Celeste when they were here. I was so worried about Brittany, if she was gonna be okay. Now…I don't know." She darted a glance in the direction of Celeste's house. "Maybe I just imagined her being like that. I mean, the whole city's acting weird, like tomorrow could be the end of everything. Still, it made no sense she didn't come out to help."

They thanked Mary Evert for her time. As they turned away, Emma couldn't help but glance at Celeste's house, wondering what secrets she was hiding from her neighbors inside her modest Craftsman.

9

Brittany and Trevor Weir's home could've been an advertisement for an HOA, with its neat lawn and hedges and picture-perfect yellow siding complemented by bright-white plantation shutters. In the dimming light of evening, the porch light glowed like a little offer of welcome.

But when a grim-faced man opened the door, even before they'd reached the front porch, Emma guessed the light had been left on out of habit rather than a beacon of hospitality.

Trevor Weir frowned at them. "We're not looking to buy, subscribe, or offer our opinions on anything. Please, go on to the next house."

Emma held her ID up, enticing him to wait even as he began to shut the door. "We're with the FBI. I'm Special Agent Emma Last."

He squinted at her through his glasses before raking a hand back through his black hair. "We already talked to the police. The guy said he wouldn't press charges. What do you want?"

Brittany Weir appeared at his shoulder, lips pinched.

Emma focused on her. "We'd like to hear your side of the

story. It's possible what you experienced is related to other recent events in and around Salem. We're not here to accuse anyone of any wrongdoing."

Wrapping an arm around Brittany, Trevor brought her forward to stand beside him in the doorway. "We're trying to put it all behind us and would appreciate you respecting our privacy."

Brittany's hand landed on his, cutting him off. "I'd like to talk to them, Trev. Okay?" Her voice sounded far stronger than she looked. "Maybe they'll know something. I want answers more than anything else."

Her husband wilted but kept his arm tight around her as he stepped back, leaving the door wide. "Come on in."

Emma led the way into a neat, open-space living room boasting navy furniture and a fireplace nested inside a brick hearth. Leo and Mia each took a seat on the oversize sectional, and Emma perched on the edge of the nearby ottoman as the Weirs sat together on the other wing of the sectional.

Brittany leaned into her husband but kept her focus on Emma. "What do you want to know?"

"Just tell us the full story." Emma glanced at Leo and Mia, who was being rubbed up on by an overly friendly tabby cat. "We'd like to hear it in your own words."

Trevor adjusted his glasses but remained silent. He frowned at his cat, as if its attitude toward Mia were traitorous. Emma assumed all cats were just attracted to black pants.

Sighing, Brittany began in a soft voice. "It happened last Sunday, a week ago tomorrow. I guess you know that. Around noon, the doorbell rang. It was a man selling solar panels. I was trying to get rid of him…

She broke off, frowning, and Trevor gripped her knee hard enough to pucker her jeans.

Leo leaned forward, tablet balanced on his thigh. "What happened at that point?"

"I got all fuzzy." Brittany pressed her fingertips to her temple. "I don't do drugs, but that's how I imagine it would feel. I couldn't think straight. My body was cold and numb, like I'd been out in the cold for hours. But it's April."

Trevor hugged her tighter. "I was still folding the laundry when I heard her stop talking mid-sentence. The guy kept going on, so I came out thinking maybe he was pushing a hard sell, you know? Brit was just standing there frozen."

"I couldn't understand what he was saying." Brittany shook her head, closing her eyes momentarily. "It was like those old Charlie Brown cartoons, where the teacher isn't meant to be understood by the audience. *Wah-wah-waaaah*, ya know? And then, I just felt this intense impulse to attack. Like my whole life would end unless I hurt him." Brittany shuddered, looking up at her husband, silently beseeching him to understand.

He hugged her closer, nodding as he spoke to Emma. "Violence is the last thing anyone would associate with Brittany. She falls apart when we lose a pet. This is our last cat of three that we had when we got married. She can't hurt a spider if it gets in the house. And even when something goes wrong, she's the calm one in the family."

A tear slid its way down Brittany's cheek. "But I've seen the video. I know what I did. I attacked him like he was threatening everything I loved." She swiped a tear away. "The next thing I knew, Trevor was pulling me off the poor guy and begging me to calm down."

She reached for the cat, and it shoved itself into Brittany's hand for affection, not an ounce of fear present.

Emma narrowed her eyes at Trevor. "Did you notice anything else?"

"After I pulled her back, she was still kinda wild." He

reached for Brittany's hand and gave it a squeeze of reassurance. "I looked at her face, trying to get her to focus on me. Her eyes were rolled back so far, I thought she was having a seizure or something. All I could see was the white part. And this'll sound nuts, but I could kinda see her pupils, like she had a film of some sort covering her eyeballs. She blinked a few times, and it was gone. And then she was just crying, and I was holding her."

She'd been pulled into the Other. But whether by Monique's doing or Celeste's is the question.

Mia hummed beneath her breath. "That must've been terrifying for both of you."

Trevor nodded. "We went to our doctor, and he ran tests earlier this week. They called yesterday and said her lab work came back normal. We have a consult with a neurologist, but they're booked for the next three months, so it'll be a while."

The cat purred, rubbing against Brittany's legs now, and she glanced up with a tired frown. "We got lucky with the salesperson, though. I didn't hurt him. Lack of practice at being violent, I guess." She forced a little hollow laugh. "He dropped the charges when Trevor promised to pay to have his pants cleaned. They got grass stains when he fell down."

"And we referred him to a friend of ours who's been looking into solar." Trevor sighed, his shoulders slumping. "Guy needs commissions more than headaches, I guess. But, yeah, that's what we can tell you. Our neighbor, Mary Evert, saw the incident, and she called it in."

Leo cleared his throat after a few seconds. "Thank you. We also want to ask about your neighbor across the way, Detective Celeste Foss. What can you tell us about her?"

Brittany jerked where she sat, staring at Leo.

"Brittany," Emma caught her eye, softening her voice,

"we're just following up on a bunch of leads and incidents. That's all. Anything you can tell us might help."

She looked at her husband, as if measuring her words, but he nodded for her to go ahead. "Well, we don't really know her. But all last week, I got the feeling she was paying more attention to us. I joked to Trevor that she was spying on us. I mean, she's a cop, and no offense, but I know suspicion comes with the job sometimes. Maybe curiosity is a better way to say it."

"What happened last week that made you think Celeste might be suspicious or curious about you?"

"Well, usually she just stays in her house when she's home." Brittany tilted her head. "But starting about a week ago, it seemed like whenever we were outside or had our garage door open, she'd be outside all of a sudden too."

"She's the lead detective on a lot of the incidents happening around town. Probably just hypervigilance." Trevor shifted sideways, cracking his neck and betraying the tension in the room. "We've always found her odd, but she handled our situation very well. Was very understanding."

Emma prodded him on with a wave. "You mentioned she was odd before. How so?"

He shook his head. "She was...she always seemed so invested in something else, barely had time to talk to any neighbors, you know? Then, after what happened with Brit, it's like we've been having Sunday dinner with her all our lives. I don't know how else to explain it."

His observation didn't fully help Emma. Suspicion and curiosity did come with the job, that was true. But the Weirs might also be misreading the actions of an observant and caring police officer.

So why didn't she come outside during the attack, then?

As Trevor talked about their neighbors, Brittany's face crumpled into tears. She looked over at Emma. "I'm sorry. I can't do this anymore. But if you find anything out, will you tell us? Please?"

"Yes." Emma stood up just as Brittany rose and hurried up the stairs, the cat clutched in her arms.

Trevor watched her go. "She's heartsick over what happened." He sighed and moved toward the door as Mia and Leo stood up from the sectional. "I'm sorry I was rude at first. If you find anything out, we'd like to know."

Leo took Trevor Weir's proffered business card and tucked it into his wallet, promising they'd be in touch if that happened. Emma gave him one in return.

He stepped between her and Mia as they headed toward the car. "Earlier, in the woods, I could describe what had happened to me as feeling fuzzy, like what Brittany Weir just said. Out of focus, like something was trying to invade my eyesight or my whole mind."

Emma paused. "That's exactly what it felt like when Monique pulled me into the Other outside Dale Grundy's cabin. Like another presence was trying to crawl into my skin and take over."

"Like the perpetrators are victims too?" Mia glanced back and forth between her colleagues.

Emma and Leo nodded, and the three of them stood in silence, staring at the ground or maybe their shoes. Anywhere but at one another.

Finally, Mia put her hands on Emma's and Leo's shoulders. "This has the potential to get way out of hand. We might want to read Jacinda in on the basics, just in case we need backup."

"None of the supernatural woo-woo stuff. We don't want our boss firing us for being lunatics." Leo rubbed his eyes, like he was trying to rub the supernatural woo-woo stuff out of his fuzzy vision.

"No, nothing about the Other."

Last Spell

"It's not a bad idea." Leo looked reluctant but in agreement.

Emma sighed and took out her phone.

Supervisory Special Agent Jacinda Hollingsworth picked up on the first ring. "Emma, how are you doing? I didn't expect to hear from you today."

"I know." She closed her eyes as Leo thumbed the key fob and they all climbed into the pearly white Malibu. Breathing in the new car smell but wishing she had an air purifier handy, Emma sat down in the passenger seat, cringing as she picked up the conversation thread with Jacinda. "Listen, I came up to Salem. I have a family matter to sort out with some old friends of my mother's. Mia and Leo came to support me."

"Everything okay? I imagine it's not, since you're calling me on a Saturday evening."

Emma smiled tightly at Jacinda's wryness and did her best to explain without brushing up against mentions of the Other. "One of my mom's friends heard I was in town and asked if I could help on a few open cases she's been struggling with. Detective Celeste Foss. We're not trying to make waves…"

"But it might happen? Or it did happen?" Jacinda muttered something to herself, though she didn't sound mad. Or entirely surprised.

"Might." Emma was quick to clarify.

"Anything I need to worry about? You all okay?"

"Yeah, we're fine." Emma shot Mia and Leo a quick thumbs-up, her stomach unclenching now that Jacinda had heard the basics and not demanded they come home. Or give her details. "I wanted to give you a heads-up, in case anyone at the Salem PD contacts you."

Jacinda sighed. "I appreciate it. Stay in touch, all right?"

Emma promised she would, then clicked off the call. She

glanced first at Mia, then at Leo, hoping she hadn't lied to Jacinda when she'd said they were fine.

She'd dragged them into this. And sure, worrying about their jobs wasn't as high stakes as worrying about their lives in a situation where the Other was involved. But she couldn't help feeling like the dangers, as well as the stakes, were growing deeper with every move she made.

Even with these last two phone calls, the little lies had felt like miniature blades of iron digging into her veins, cold and narrow and hard.

10

Emma glanced at Leo, remembering he'd been talking before she called Jacinda. "You were saying how you felt 'fuzzy' in the woods before we visited Monique. Like Brittany?"

He opened the driver's door. "I think we have more to worry about than me being off my game for a few seconds. Let's just focus on what's in front of us now." He put one foot inside the vehicle and paused. He shook himself and stepped back, standing in the street.

"Leo? Everything okay over there?"

"You know what? No, it's not." He slammed the car door. "Weren't we going to talk to Celeste? Whose idea was it to drive off?"

Emma flashed a look at Mia, who appeared just as confused as she was. "Nobody said to drive anywhere."

"We hadn't discussed where we were going yet." Mia chewed her lip.

He rubbed his eyes. When he pulled his hands away, they were sunken and red. "Must be this day catching up with me. I feel like I could either pass out or run a marathon."

What the hell does that mean?

Before Emma could ask him to explain, Leo thumbed the fob to lock the car and came around to join them on the sidewalk. "How do you want to do this?"

Emma stared at him. She wanted to hit rewind and get some clarity about his sudden shift in mood, but Mia beat her to the punch, drawing everyone's attention back to the moment.

"We have nothing to confront Celeste about, even after talking to her neighbors. If we believe she's involved in what's happening, she hasn't done anything that's technically against the law."

"Assault and battery?" Emma wanted to call out the criminal incidents, but they were on very shaky ground.

Leo shifted between them, yawning before he spoke again. "There are laws against coercing or manipulating people into acts of violence. Her using magic to do so, assuming she's the guilty party, would be like magic roofies. Different means, same end."

"Prove it in court, Ambrose." Emma didn't know if speaking to the woman was the right move at this point or worth their time at all. "If she's really behind this and wants me to believe otherwise, why would she commit crimes so close to her own home? She's basically painting a target on her front door, and that doesn't make a ton of sense."

Mia sighed. "You're right. It would make a lot more sense for Monique to have staged all this to implicate Celeste. She could've reached out to you to throw suspicion off her. Criminals inserting themselves into a case is nothing new."

"*Trust Celeste* column, check." Leo made a check mark in the air.

Emma gritted her teeth. She wasn't ready to paint Monique as the villain yet. Suspicion was one thing, and she had plenty of that for both of her mom's old friends. "Criminals presenting themselves as victims is also not a new tactic. It's possible that Celeste is arrogant enough to think we'd never see through her ruse."

Leo ran a hand through his unruly hair. "We're going in circles. The only way we find out anything else is to just go talk to the woman."

Without waiting for a reply, he stormed across the street, aiming for Celeste's house. They hurried to catch up.

At the curb, Emma couldn't help pausing. Unlike Monique's cabin, Celeste lived in a nondescript, almost bland Craftsman home. The facade appeared dreary and unwelcoming, with the shades all drawn closed, and the dark-gray paint set it further apart from its neighbors. Twin flower boxes hung beneath the front windows, offering the only glimmer of color.

She's a cop who doesn't have time to do much decorating.

Emma's own apartment often felt like a lot to take care of in her line of work.

She marched up the walk, half expecting the paving stones she stepped on to sink into the ground. But they reached the porch without incident.

The door opened the instant Emma's knuckles connected with the wood.

Celeste had been waiting.

The other two greeted her as Emma watched, a tightness building in her chest. She cleared her throat, drawing the white-haired woman's gaze back to her. "We were hoping you might be able to tell us about what happened with your neighbor Brittany Weir."

Celeste's brown eyes remained flat, though one eyebrow puckered up. "Do you want my cop opinion or my personal opinion?"

"Personal."

"I think you already know what I have to say on the matter, but I don't mind coming right out with it. I believe

Brittany committed assault and battery under Monique's supernatural influence."

Mia took in an audible breath at Emma's back.

Emma watched the woman closely. "Someone mentioned they saw you smiling that day, during the attack."

"I wouldn't dream of it. I take my job very seriously. I protect this neighborhood, this city." Celeste closed her mouth and took in a deep breath in an apparent attempt to calm her outrage. "If someone thought I was smiling...well, perhaps they mistook the lines on my old face for something else."

Emma avoided rolling her eyes, but just barely. There was not a line on Celeste's face.

"I was...for want of a better word...*concentrating*. Trying to help." She reached out, her hand hovering just over Emma's arm. "But I can't stop her alone, which is why we need to work together."

Leo shifted beside her, and Emma got the impression he wanted to leave the porch then and there. She did too.

"If you feel that way," Emma measured her words, "why didn't you try to get in touch with me like Monique did? Why not come to me and tell me we needed to be working together, before anything got out of hand here?"

Celeste looked quizzical. "Why on earth would I risk your safety that way? I only asked you for help recently because you're already here. I figured, kill two birds with one stone. By keeping you close, I could protect you, and by getting your help, I could get to know you while also stopping Monique forever."

Before Emma could digest that newest argument, Celeste switched her attitude. "Would you all like to come in? I can make tea or coffee."

"We can't." Emma stepped back, nearly running into Mia behind her. "Maybe another time."

The slightest frown of disappointment—or anger—furrowed Celeste's otherwise flawless brow.

"Have a good night, then. Don't let the Salem bedbugs bite. I hope to see you tomorrow, and we can talk about these cases under less emotionally charged circumstances." On that note, Celeste shut the door.

Emma remained facing the door, even as she backed down the steps of the porch, expecting something more to happen. But the door stayed closed.

"Nice parting wish." Leo shivered visibly.

Emma couldn't tell if the motion was for effect or if he truly felt shaken. "Let's get out of here."

11

Officer Edward Holden shifted in the roller chair behind his desk, observing the large man in the holding cell to his right. Damien Knight had been a gentle giant since they'd picked him up. Now, however, he paced his cell, gripping his unruly hair, muttering to himself nonstop.

Edward's chair creaked under his weight as he shifted to take in the rest of the office. His partner, Michael Konig, sat at his desk, which faced Edward's, but he was obscured by his computer monitor.

Michael typed madly on his keyboard in between scrolling on whatever websites he was browsing.

"You okay over there, Mike? Maybe it's time to take a breather, get off the social media roller coaster." Michael was addicted to doomscrolling. He always knew the latest and worst things going on anywhere in the world, but usually took it in stride. He was a good officer.

But his behavior tonight was different, unlike anything Edward had seen in him before.

Michael didn't reply. Just kept scrolling and pounding on the keys.

"Mike, you in there? I said maybe it's time—"

"Heard you just fine, Ed. There's no end in sight. Weird shit keeps on coming down the wire." Michael shoved back from his desk and started pacing. "What are we supposed to do here? That housewife, she lights into a salesperson for no reason. Knight over there," he aimed a thumb at the cell, "goes ballistic and kills his neighbor. Strangles her after years of treating her like a grandmother."

Edward waved a hand at Michael's woes. "Brittany Weir's charges were dropped. Probably because the salesperson was hitting on her like a creep and wasn't ready for her to hit back."

"What about Knight?" Michael stopped in front of the cell, his back to Knight. "He has a heart of gold, maybe." He turned around to face their prisoner. "Hey, Knight, you got a heart of gold?"

The man continued to worry his hair with both hands as he paced his cell. That was all the evidence Edward needed to know Knight had reached some kind of limit he wasn't coming back from anytime soon.

Edward shrugged. "If you ask me, I think he snapped. A guy needs something to keep him going in life. Something more than just work and being a good neighbor. We should be happy he didn't go on a shooting spree." He gazed at the clock on the wall, wishing Michael would sit down or go get coffee.

Michael just stood there, staring.

Edward stood and stepped around his desk toward his partner. "Hey, Mike, how about you grab us something from the gas station down the block? I could go for a turkey and Swiss from their fridge, and their coffee's better than ours." He reached for his wallet. "I'll treat—"

"It's not going to stop!" Damien Knight went stock-still in his cell, facing the back wall. His words were suddenly clear and echoing as he repeated them. "It's not going to stop."

Both officers froze with their hands hovering over their weapons.

"What's he talking about?" Edward stepped closer.

"Got me." Michael leaned toward the bars. "Hey, Knight. What's not gonna stop?"

The man twisted around at the waist, with his feet still anchored to the floor of his cell. He stared over his left shoulder at them.

His eyes had gone white.

Edward's stomach flipped at the sight, and he remembered the description Trevor Weir had given of his wife. He'd written it off as a *heat of the moment* hallucination, all nerves and no reality. But Damien Knight's eyes were unnaturally white, as if made of marble. His hands clenched and unclenched in a repeated rhythm.

Suddenly, he was damn glad the man was locked in a cell and only wished there were more officers in the station for backup.

"You seeing this, too, or am I losing it?" Edward's voice cracked, and a quick heat of embarrassment rose in his cheeks. Any man in his right mind would be disturbed right now. "Mike? Hey, Konig, did you hear me?"

What in the ever-loving shit?

Michael had gone as still as their prisoner. He wavered on his feet, both hands hovering around his pockets now.

"Mike! What the—"

Michael muttered to himself, plucking up the key ring off his belt and directing a single key toward the cell door.

Bile rose in Edward's throat. His partner's movements were jerky, like he was intoxicated.

Michael fit the key into the cell door and opened it.

Edward drew his weapon. "Officer Konig! Stand down and step away from the cell door."

He brought his gun up and aimed it at Knight, who pushed past Michael. He appeared equally as intoxicated and off-kilter as he approached Edward.

"Hold it right there, Knight. You take one more step, I will shoot."

Neither men said anything coherent.

Edward backed up, putting the desks between him and the other two men. "Konig! Get your head on straight. Put some cuffs on the prisoner. Do something, dammit!"

Michael went back to his desk and picked up a pair of cuffs.

Finally, you dumbass.

With his gun trained on Knight's center mass, Edward repeated his order to stand down. "Stay where you are, Knight. Now turn and place your hands on the wall beside you. Stand with your feet apart. Last chance. You take one more step, I will shoot."

The man struggled, as if fighting to control his own movements. His foot lifted and went back down in the same place. Knight's hands continued to clench and unclench at his sides. His pupils were nowhere to be seen. Was this a seizure?

Edward kept his aim on the large man's chest and called to his partner. "Konig, you got them cuffs?"

Michael came around the other side of the desks to stand at Edward's left side. Edward turned to face his partner and nearly jumped out of his own skin. Michael's eyes were the same milky white as Knight's.

"Mike?"

The first cuff went around Edward's left wrist. He swung around, trying to shake Michael's grip, but another set of hands grabbed him from the right.

Michael twisted his gun away and threw it on the desk. He and Knight seized Edward and slammed him against the wall. They began chanting what Knight had said in the cell like it was some kind of prayer. Their voices echoed in unison as Edward's heart jackhammered in his chest.

"It's not going to stop. It's not going to stop."

"Mike, what the hell? Let me go. Mike!"

Knight's hands shot up, wrapping around Edward's throat. Glaring at him with those ghostly eyes, he squeezed. Edward batted at his face, pushing his jaw to the side and trying desperately to bring a knee up where it might do some good. But he only had one hand. Michael had the other cuffed and was wrestling to take him down too.

He tried to wedge his right hand between Knight's, hoping to force the man's grip to break. But he was losing oxygen, getting weaker by the second.

Michael, holding tight to his cuffed wrist, spoke. "It's not going to stop, Ed. Not now, not ever. She wants more."

"Who?" He could barely squeak the word out.

Knight's two hands were like a retracting metal vise around his neck. The man was a beast with almost superhuman strength. He kept squeezing until the burning in Edward's lungs was accompanied by the deafening pop of some bone in his throat. A stabbing pain shot down his spine and up through his jaw. His temples pounded, gasping gurgles coming out of his lips as Knight squeezed tighter.

In the corner of Edward's narrowing, weakening vision, Michael was nodding, eyes as blank as Knight's. "She wants more."

Edward's free hand slipped from Knight's arm, falling uselessly to his side. The weight in his chest pressed harder, unbearable now. His pulse thundered in his ears, fading into the cold whisper of her name. He didn't know who *she* was or what *she* wanted—but she'd taken him.

12

Tree branches arched over my clearing, forming a canopy that blocked out the sun. A chill, more like autumn than late spring, hung in the air. Whispers from the Other curled around me like spectral fingers. Those spirits couldn't touch me, however. No matter how much a few of them might want to get their creepy hands around my throat.

I circled the ground a couple times before dropping myself onto the grass. Crisscross applesauce, like the three of us used to sit when we first discovered the Place of Moonlight. Monique, Gina, and Celeste—the three musketeers, the three *amigas*, and sometimes, the three stooges.

But the Place of Moonlight was weak compared to my clearing.

This place was mine. All mine, now that Gina was gone.

My liminal realm, where the dead lingered.

Where power could be centered.

"And you've got to recenter yourself, girl. It's all coming along as planned. Don't lose focus now."

Seeing Emma Last, all grown up, had thrown me more

than I'd anticipated. She looked so much like Gina, my Gina before she'd betrayed me. They shared the same sky-blue eyes and quizzical expression, as if they were constantly trying to figure something out.

And they shared something else…the power that should've remained solely with me once Gina chose to marry and have a child.

I'd expected anger and fury when I saw that child, Emma. I had not prepared myself to want to hug her. The ache to wrap my arms around her, the way I'd wrapped them around her mother so long ago. Gina had been my soul sister. Family had been a foreign concept until she walked into my life.

Before I met my "sisters," I was always the freak, the loner who never had a friend. The quiet one in the corner no one seemed to understand. Maybe I was too quiet. Whatever it was, no one liked me. I collected little cruelties like other girls collected friendship bracelets.

"She's weird."

"What's she wearing?"

"Scoot your chair over. Don't let her sit by us."

And then, Gina. Bright, shining Gina came into my life. When she was young, she was rather plain. Pretty enough not to be offensive but not intimidating, so she drew neither attention nor ire. If I fell into the pretty category, I hadn't known it at the time. I wore hand-me-downs. My hair was unevenly cut, and I looked a little shaggy. But my skin was clear.

Gina saw beyond the frizzy, crooked bangs. Beyond my social inadequacies. We met after some queen bee—whose name I couldn't remember—pushed an empty chair away from the lunch table so I couldn't sit next to her. Gina glared at the girl before touching my arm…

"Follow me." She'd carried the chair to a nearby table, where another girl was eating alone.

Everybody had introduced themselves, and I'd sat down. Then Gina had sat next to me.

After that, the three of us were inseparable.

Gina made us feel cherished. Chosen. I mattered for the first time ever.

I had a place in this world. A home, crafted not of walls and a roof but of secrets whispered in the dark at sleepovers, of fingers intertwined as we walked through the zoo, of genuine laughter ringing out over the other bitches' derisive comments at nearby tables. Gina filled up all the aching, empty places inside each of us. She was a special person with normal parents, and it showed.

I drew in a deep breath, letting the pine scent and fresh earth infiltrate my lungs. When I exhaled, my mind went to a darker place.

When Gina announced her engagement to that *man*, I'd tasted ashes in my mouth. She came back to us for a time, and I thought we might still maintain the bond we'd pledged to uphold with our blood.

Instead, she announced her pregnancy. She forsook our craft, our destiny, for a life of mundane domesticity that didn't include us. Gina left the trinity of sisters we had formed, for a husband...and then a child.

"Emma."

Her name was a knife in my ribs.

When I first discovered Emma's existence, my thoughts had been a whirlwind of rage and terror. Rage for the betrayal she represented. Terror for the uncertainty her existence would create.

Now that I knew her and had seen how much of Gina's vitality the girl had been granted...I felt that attraction we used to have all over again. I missed my friend more than ever. I missed those teenage years. They were the best of my life. I wanted to hug Emma. That was my first instinct.

Which enraged me. I had to swallow that urge and the anger it created every time I saw her now.

When Gina had been with us, we'd spoken of the Other as "our place," and the hours we spent interacting with Shades had given me such a feeling of strength and agency. When we were apart, I'd been hollow.

I had to be clever. This Emma girl was sharp. I couldn't strike at her directly. Not yet.

The protective magic surrounding her would fight me. I needed the girl to trust me, to steer me to my first adversary—the one who'd cast the protective spell. Without removing her, I couldn't get to Gina's daughter.

Seeing Emma and her colleagues together had also sent me into an emotional spiral. The three of them, teamed up together, unified in their goals. I had that once.

Gina's spawn took it all away.

Emma deserved to have her found family taken away from her too. I would take what she loved most in the world away before ending her. This was the only way she'd ever understand what kind of pain she'd inflicted upon me.

I paused with a hand over my heart, feeling the weight of loss and emptiness. All the death, all the manipulation, would soon come to an end. My power, my legacy, would be secured for all time.

The Other called me. I had work to do beyond the veil.

I tilted my head back, filled my lungs and howled.

13

Gordon Bronson and his golden retriever, Raimi, stopped near an old oak at the edge of his neighborhood. They hadn't been on a good long walk for the past week, not since some woman down the block attacked a door-to-door salesperson in broad daylight. Between that incident and all the other trouble around the city, Gordon was about ready to pull up stakes.

But he couldn't leave the city of his birth. The city where he hit his first home run in Little League, where he founded an after-school reading program. Fell in love, started a family.

And where he found Raimi as a stray puppy.

The old golden sniffed around the oak tree, nose nuzzling into the earth.

Gordon smiled. "I know, old buddy, I know. Summer's just around the corner, and there's all sorts of aromas blooming up all over for you to enjoy."

The dog ignored him.

One of these days, he'll get a snout-full of fire ants if he's not careful.

Peering around the neighborhood, Gordon allowed the dog to take his time as he kept an eye out. The morning was still peaceful. These walks had become ritual since the dog had come into his life. But lately, Gordon chose to come out earlier and earlier, just to ensure he had the streets to himself. His community had been positively untethered in recent weeks.

The chaos made him thankful to work from home, but it was only in these early mornings when he could leave the house and still feel relaxed. Molly and the children were at home in bed. Safe.

And Raimi appreciated the walks. He might have a decent-sized backyard at home, but every dog liked to do a bit of territory tracking.

Finally, the dog lifted a leg, and Gordon turned to face the direction from which they'd come to consider their route home. Two houses down, a man swayed on his feet as he stumbled along the sidewalk, then wandered straight into the street. He had something in one hand, but Gordon couldn't make it out.

The man staggered in a circle, right in the middle of the road, before returning to the sidewalk.

Gordon watched him steady himself against a car parked along the curb. He seemed drunk or high on something. Probably had a bottle in his hand. Had to be, the way he kept using his free hand to swat at his head like he wanted to knock some sense into himself.

If that ain't a sign of the times, I don't know what is. Whole dang city of Salem is coming undone, and it's lost causes like that one who're to blame.

He'd worked as an occupational therapist for years and had helped people who had all sorts of maladies and conditions that made their lives difficult. Plenty had come to him after trying to self-medicate their aches, pains, and frustrations.

Drugs and drink never did anything but make life worse.

Up ahead, the man wavered where he stood, then found his balance and started heading in Gordon's direction.

"Sir, are you all right? Do you need me to call an ambulance?"

Raimi whined beside him and turned away from the approaching figure, in the opposite direction of home.

Gordon knew dogs could sense danger, so he turned away from the man, too, to take the long way back to Molly and the kids. "Come on, Raimi. Let's get you home to your breakfast and—"

The pounding of footsteps on the sidewalk behind him caused the rest of the sentence to die in his throat. Turning to look over his shoulder, he spotted the man barreling in his direction, and he got a good look at his face.

This was the man on the news just the day before. The man who'd killed an old woman without reason. As scary as that was, the hatchet hanging in the man's right hand was even more terrifying.

It sent a cold shiver down his spine, and Raimi growled, low and deep in a way that he'd never heard from the dog before.

Gordon turned and ran, with the axe-wielding maniac's footsteps echoing on the pavement behind them.

"Leave us alone!" Gordon and his retriever kept running, side by side. "We've done nothing to you!"

Raimi let out a dire howl and spun around, halting Gordon in his tracks, lest the leash be torn from his hand. A sudden, searing pain split his back and shot down his left side.

He spun, his arms outstretched, both his hands empty. The pain in Gordon's back grew heavier, thicker.

He threw that hatchet. He threw it and hit me in the back.

The reality of his situation settled into Gordon like the blade that had embedded itself in his back. Pressure built in his chest with each painful breath.

Distantly, he knew Raimi was attacking the man. He could hear it. Gordon fell to his knees, straining to see his attacker and his beloved golden retriever. They were nowhere.

He collapsed onto his side and glimpsed the two of them tangled up on a neighbor's lawn. Somewhere, a door slammed. A man screamed. Raimi barked and growled savagely.

Gordon's eyes closed against the burning agony of the hatchet in his back. His breathing grew ragged and short. Each inhalation seemed to pull the blade deeper into his body.

He sensed someone close to him and hesitantly opened his eyes.

The man who'd thrown the hatchet was there, towering over him. His eyes were blank, empty, and white.

Like a statue. He looks like a statue, and the sculptor forgot to paint his eyes.

The giant clamped his hands around Gordon's neck, squeezing the air from him. His lips began moving, like he was being forced to speak against his own will. "I'm sorry. I'm sorry. She wants more. I'm sorry."

Tears slipped from Gordon's eyes as the pain in his back was replaced with a scorching pressure in his chest. He couldn't breathe, and his vision tunneled. His ears filled with the sound of Raimi's frantic barking.

Gordon's lungs burned. He wanted to scream at Raimi to run, but the dog kept barking.

The man above him reached around with one hand and

pulled out the hatchet, while he continued to choke Gordon with his other hand.

The last thing Gordon saw was the hatchet blade, slick and dark with his own blood, coming down toward the side of his neck.

14

Emma blinked into the bright light of the room. A persistent banging had intruded her dreams. She shook off the night and pulled herself from bed to answer her hotel room door.

"I'm coming!" She nearly tripped over her boots as she brushed a hurried hand through her hair. She straightened her sweatshirt and confirmed she had pajama bottoms on before peering through the peephole. It had been a long night with little sleep.

She yawned as she stepped back and yanked open the door to Mia and Leo. Mia was on the phone, and Leo was poised to knock again.

"Good morning."

He rolled his eyes. "Or something like that."

Leo led the way inside as Mia tucked her phone away. She pointed to Emma's phone on the nightstand. "I tried calling."

"Sorry. Sleepless night."

"You and me both. Anybody hear howling outside the hotel?" Leo looked from woman to woman.

"What?" Emma and Mia exchanged a confused look.

"All I'm saying is, I didn't get much sleep, either, and I'm ready to go."

Emma waved off Leo's comment and his questioning look at all the extra blankets tucked around the bed like a giant bird's nest. "Yeah, okay. So what's going on?"

Mia moved over to the curtains and pulled them wide, flooding the room with light. "I just got a call from Detective Foss. She says they've had two more murders."

Two? Dammit.

"When and where?"

"The first was at the police station, last night around ten o'clock."

Emma blinked, squinting through the fresh sunlight. "The police station? Someone was killed *there*?"

"By Damien Knight." Leo perched on the edge of the bed, fiddling with the medal he wore around his neck, betraying his nerves. "The officer we met, Michael Konig, let Knight out of his cell without any clear reason and assisted as Knight killed another officer, Edward Holden. All of it happened on video. Konig's and Knight's eyes were both empty, all white."

"They've been arrested, right?"

Mia shook her head. "Detective Foss put out an APB for both men. They were last seen in a police cruiser, and dispatch can't confirm the vehicle's location. The GPS tracker was disabled."

Sitting heavily on the opposite side of the bed from Leo, Emma folded in on herself. The Other was being weaponized against innocent people, turning them into helpless automatons. And now a police officer was dead. "Was the second victim also a cop?"

"No." Mia sighed. "The second victim was killed in a suburb about two hours ago. Neighbors heard yelling outside and a dog barking."

"What happened?"

"I didn't get details, but it sounds like it was Knight again. Detective Foss has initiated a manhunt going for him and Konig. At this point, though, they could be anywhere."

Leo stood and smoothed his pants, heading for the door. "Her department is already stretched to the breaking point. None of this is making her job any easier."

"Where are you going?"

She and Mia both looked at him as he stood by the door, hand on the knob and his back turned to them. "I'll get us some breakfast sandwiches and coffee at the drive-through next door. We'll need it."

He left, closing the door softly behind him.

"What the hell's gotten into Leo?" Emma got up and began digging clothes out of her suitcase, looking for a fresh pair of socks.

"No idea, but I wouldn't mind having the old Ambrose back. Do you think he's struggling to accept all this and is just playing along?"

"No." Emma shook her head firmly. "He believes me just as much as you do."

"I hope so. We all need to be on the same page if we want to help Detective Foss and the rest of Salem."

Assuming Celeste is the one we should be trying to help.

By the time they'd gotten outside and downstairs, Leo was zipping back across the parking lot. He pulled to the curb beside them. Emma ducked inside and was chomping into a sizzling sausage biscuit a moment later.

Mia read off the address of the most recent crime scene, and Leo punched it into the GPS. They drove mostly in silence, save for the sounds of chewing and Leo nearly gagging on the coffee.

"Next time, we wake up early enough to find good coffee. In fact, I plan on waking up early every morning until we're done here, just to be safe." He smacked his lips, as if that would get rid of the extreme bitter taste.

Leo drove them across a narrow bridge that spanned a simple water feature to Gordon Bronson's suburb. They passed between two decorative low walls, announcing "Monarch Glen," and took the first left onto the neighborhood street where the crime had occurred.

Sirens pealed from behind them as a black-and-white whipped around their Malibu. The patrol car sped forward and swerved to stop across both lanes of traffic, creating a barricade and cutting them off.

A curse slipped from Leo's lips as he slammed on the brakes. Coffee splashed out of Emma's cup, burning her legs.

"What the hell?" Emma glared at the black-and-white.

"Unbelievable. If he thinks I'm gonna let this slide as some stupid mistake…" Leo tugged out his badge, scowling.

Like Leo, Emma thought maybe this was a case of mistaken identity—an overzealous officer trying to prevent civilians from approaching a crime scene. But then the officer stepped out of the cruiser.

It was Michael Konig.

He moved awkwardly, as if struggling with an injury to his back or leg as he moved toward the rear of his cruiser. After a few jerky steps, he spun back to stand by the driver's door. Konig then shook his head and swatted at his ears before going still like a statue.

Leo leaned forward over the wheel. "What the hell is he doing?"

Konig pivoted to face them, and a sudden gust of Other chill washed over Emma.

"Mia, you said Konig let Knight out of his cell and they both killed Edward Holden."

"That's what Celeste said." Mia tapped at her phone. "I'm texting her now."

"Maybe he's come back to himself. If he's being influenced by *whatever*, the shift back to normal is sudden, right? That's what happened with Brittany." Leo settled back in his seat, but kept the car on, his full attention on the officer. "You said Knight was grief-stricken when you spoke to him. Could be Konig is back in his right mind, regretting his actions and coming to us for…well, not absolution, but support. Or something like it."

"Let's hope you're right." Emma took a deep breath, wondering if she could talk through this confrontation with Konig. Her hope wasn't high. "Even if he was under some magical influence from last night, he hasn't exactly been Mr. Sunshine any of the times we've spoken. Normal Konig might not be much better than the alternative."

Nevertheless, she opened her door, ready to give it a try.

Konig's shoulder dipped at the sound, and his hand came up with his service weapon aimed at them.

Emma had one foot outside the vehicle and no time to process what Konig was doing when Leo gripped her belt and yanked her back inside. A bullet skated off the top of their Malibu.

Emma ducked in her seat as Leo put the vehicle in reverse and sped backward down the street. More bullets tore into the vehicle's hood, and the windshield spider-webbed in one corner.

"You going to give us some cover fire?" Leo shot the question at Emma as he reversed. They fishtailed until Leo spun them around a corner.

"He's not himself. Someone else is doing this." She deeply didn't want to kill the man. "I try really hard not to shoot at innocent people unless I can help it."

Konig followed them on foot several yards before stopping in the middle of the intersection and firing until he was out of bullets. All three agents ducked toward the floorboards, Leo's head barely poking above the steering wheel. Konig was a lousy shot. The bullets went wide.

Leo slammed on the brakes, and Emma was out of the car and sprinting toward Konig a second later with Leo on her heels. When she reached Konig, he'd recovered enough to slot another magazine into place.

He lifted the weapon.

"Shit." Emma slid to a halt.

Konig's left hand reached over his body, clawing at his right arm, trying to pull it back. He wasn't aiming at her yet.

He's fighting with himself. He doesn't want to kill us.

"Officer Konig, stand down. Release the weapon and stand down."

Leo was at her side. His weapon was drawn, but he had the same internal struggle she did. They couldn't fire on him. He wasn't responsible for his actions.

Konig stared at them, shaking his head. His eyes glimmered a ghostly white.

"Michael. Michael, fight it." Emma couldn't tell if her words were getting through or not. "Don't listen to her. Whatever she's saying, she's a liar."

But which her?

"You hear me?" Emma shouted at whoever was controlling the officer. "You're lying to him. Let him go!"

Konig managed to wrestle with his right arm, but he wasn't winning. The muzzle swung between Leo and Emma. She couldn't decide the best angle to help.

Leo sucked in a breath. "He's under her control. She forced him to let Knight escape."

"We have to flank him. It's the only way one of us will get close enough to take him down safely."

As if hearing her plan, Konig's arm jerked up like a marionette and brought the gun to the side of his head.

Emma rushed forward. "No! Don't!"

He fired, and a gout of blood and brain matter erupted onto the street. By the time his lifeless body hit the ground, Konig's eyes had faded from white back to brown.

Leo stared down at the dead man. "Fuck. Fuck, fuck, fuck."

Mia took fast, deep breaths beside Emma. She was about to say something when a sudden volley of gunfire erupted from deeper in the suburb. "That's the direction we were heading."

Leo holstered his gun. "Call this in. I'll move his cruiser so we can get by."

"How about you use the cruiser's radio and call for backup?" Emma swallowed against the angry bile rising in her throat.

"I'll do that and check out what's happening up ahead. You two secure the scene." Leo pointed down the street.

Mia nodded. "I'll come with—"

Waving her off, he took off at a sprint and was at the downed cop's vehicle within seconds. "Stay here with Emma to keep control of this scene and the body. Keys are in the Malibu!"

The shot-up Malibu with a nearly shattered windshield. Great.

Emma gulped air, fighting to regain control of her thoughts as Leo dropped into the cruiser's driver's seat, backed up, and sped off. "He's driving fast, for him."

Mia punched her in the shoulder and not lightly. "You're joking right now? Seriously?"

Shaking her head, Emma crouched by the body. "I don't know what I'm doing. But I do know we have to call Jacinda. This is getting out of hand in a big way."

"What are you going to tell her?"

Emma had no idea, but her phone was against her ear and already ringing.

Jacinda answered quickly. "Emma. Thank God."

"Hey, we—"

"Are in the middle of a shit show." Jacinda spoke fast, and a horn honked in the background as she put the phone on speaker. "It's all over the news. A cop was murdered last night."

Emma glanced down at the body. "There are two cops down now. One just tried to shoot us, and then he shot himself before we could stop him."

The line remained silent for a few seconds before Jacinda muttered something to someone on her end. Whoever answered Jacinda sounded a lot like Vance. Emma hoped he was ready for work after his head injury. It was just like him to push too hard.

Emma and Mia stepped out of the street and onto the sidewalk just as Leo pulled up alongside them, window down. Emma held up her phone and mouthed Jacinda's name.

Leo got out of the cruiser, leaning close to the speaker.

"This is a crazy. We just got an official ask for assistance from the Boston office. I need you to go offer support to the nearest responding Agency."

"Jacinda, this is Leo." He took a deep breath before continuing. "There's no responding Agency at this point. I was just near another murder scene. We have a couple houses on fire too."

"What about calling the station? Are they not responding by radio?"

"I was going to," Leo gave Emma and Mia a grim look, "but Konig used a tire iron to smash the radio in this vehicle. He left the iron on the passenger seat."

Emma turned in a circle, searching for any sign of attackers or authorities. The only movement was a curtain tugged sideways, no doubt to hide some curious onlooker's presence before they could approach.

Jacinda cursed loudly enough that Emma flinched. "Find someone with authority there and follow their lead. That's all we can do right now. I'll call again once I have direction from higher up."

Ending the call, Emma walked back into the street to stand by Konig's body. She crouched and stared at the dead man's dead eyes. "They're not white anymore."

A hand squeezed her shoulder. It was Leo, with Mia by his side. "We have to figure out which woman is doing this."

Mia's phone buzzed. "Jacinda just texted. She's sending help."

"That won't stop anything. It might even make things worse. We're running out of time to figure this out."

Salem was turning into a war zone, and they were the only ones who even had a clue what was truly happening. Worse…who would believe them if they tried to explain?

15

Emma confirmed Jacinda's text on her phone before slipping the device into her pocket, looking up as another black-and-white pulled to the curb.

Let's hope this officer's in their own mind, Emma girl.

The door opened even before the engine turned off, and a large middle-aged man stepped out, his day's worth of stubble a few shades darker than his deep brown skin. He stomped their way without looking at them, focused on the corpse of Officer Michael Konig.

Leo had pulled a sheet from the cruiser's trunk, and they'd used that to cover Konig. Emma couldn't avert her gaze from the dark stain creeping outward on the asphalt.

The approaching cop squatted and lifted the sheet, revealing Konig's dead face. "I'm Chief of Police Earl Peterson. Detective Foss gave me the short version. You want to give me the full story here?"

Emma filled him in while he examined their credentials, though his focus kept returning to Konig's body.

"I didn't want to believe it when Detective Foss called. Your story matches what she told me. After what happened with his partner and Knight, I guess I can't be surprised. Whatever's in the water around here, it's killing people."

Emma nodded, allowing the man space to observe his downed officer.

Mia stepped up to the chief, speaking quietly. "Is he an isolated incident? Have any other officers started acting… odd?"

Chief Peterson grimaced. "He's not the only cop who's come close to crossing the line or stepping all the way over it, but he's the only one who's attempted murder or…taken himself out."

Raising one hand to rub his stubble, the man closed his eyes for a moment. Chief Peterson looked more stressed than anyone Emma had seen in recent memory, with red-rimmed eyes she guessed added ten years to his age.

Finally, he faced away from Konig and drew himself straighter. "Officer Vales is on her way. She'll act as Incident Commander here."

Emma held out her gun. "Would you like to collect our weapons, pending your investigation of this incident?"

He looked from her gun to her face and back again. "Did you fire it?"

"No."

"Then no. We can use all the help we can get…there's no denying it. I'll trust you to shoot only if you have to. Just make sure we touch base before you leave town." Peterson turned to go but paused. "You were headed to the crime scene where Gordon Bronson was killed. Still going there?"

"We'd like to take a look, if that's possible." Emma gestured in the direction Leo had gone earlier. "We heard there are fires in the area, though…"

"Yeah. I was dealing with another fire across town, or I would've been here sooner." He waved down a black-and-white that had turned into the suburb. Officer Sandra Vales was at the wheel. Before she'd gotten out of the car, the chief nodded toward their shot-up Malibu. "If that thing's still drivable, you can follow me over to the Bronson crime scene. My people say they got the area under control, so it should be safe now."

After following Chief Peterson into the suburb, Leo parked behind the chief's cruiser, and Emma got out. She didn't know what they'd be able to determine from a crime scene influenced by mind control, but she wouldn't give up on following what procedures remained to them.

Meeting Mia at the front of the vehicle, she set off toward a trio of cops standing around a bloodied sheet that had been draped over the victim's remains.

"Shit." Leo stepped up beside them as one of the cops drew the sheet away to reveal Gordon Bronson's mutilated corpse.

Chief Peterson motioned to the body. "If you want to help, you can start by figuring out what the hell this is all about." He shook his head and walked away, heading toward a second huddle of his officers.

Emma only stared at the victim's remains. Gordon Bronson had been killed, she hoped, by a slice through his neck and upper torso. But all four of his limbs had been severed. His arms were in two pieces, cut below the elbow. His legs had each been savagely amputated below the knee.

Whistling slowly, Leo stood up. "This is next-level. More than mere escalation. The first two victims died by strangulation."

Mia held a hand over her mouth and turned from the body. "It would've been really hard for Knight to commit all three murders by himself. It looks like one of our women can control more than one person at a time."

Leo, apparently, had the same thought. "She must've been controlling Konig. He was with Knight when Officer Holden was killed. He provided an escape in the cruiser they stole from the station. And his eyes were white."

Staring at Gordon's remains, Emma took a moment to settle her nerves. They'd arrived at a town on the edge of chaos, and now she felt like a thunderstorm had suddenly rolled in on top of her.

Mia put a hand on her arm. "Emma? You okay?"

She nodded, still staring at Gordon's mauled corpse. "Reminds me of Little Clementine."

Leo stepped closer and whispered in her ear. "I know you saw the victims on that case, sometimes while the crime scene was still being processed. Any chance Gordon the ghost is around here somewhere?"

She'd expected the same thing but had, so far, seen no ghosts or Shades or whatever they were called. She also hadn't felt the chill of the Other around them. "Nothing yet."

Chief Peterson returned. "I have people searching for Damien Knight, and I'm in touch with the mayor's office. Because of the random fires, we're putting out a shelter-in-place order for the whole city. That'll help, I hope."

The air around Emma turned cold. She looked to the other side of the street, where a golden retriever sat whining at the end of a leash held by an officer.

Nearby, she spotted Gordon Bronson's ghost. He stared down at the dog sadly.

His transparent severed limbs reminded Emma of Ned Logan's decapitated head. Gordon's mouth moved as his head hung limply to one side, revealing the depth of the cut that had killed him.

Whatever magic Celeste or Monique had used to possess Knight, violence was emphasized over anything else. Gordon mouthed some words, but Emma couldn't hear them. She took a few careful steps closer, pausing when Gordon's voice became clear over the surrounding chatter and distant sirens.

"I hope you walk near the trees, Raimi." Gordon's ghost leaned down, petting the dog with a see-through hand. "You'll have plenty of nice smells to explore there."

Leo stepped in beside her, frowning at the retriever. "He was walking his dog when he was attacked. They're going to get him back to the family as soon as they confirm there's no evidence on him."

Without responding or attempting to engage with the ghost, Emma moved with Leo back toward Mia and the chief.

Chief Peterson nodded at her and Leo, one hand back on his stubble, scratching with irritation. "Special Agent Logan here tells me your SSA in D.C. is on her way with reinforcements. I asked the Bureau to send whoever they can, and we have mutual support inbound from Boston. Massport is sending some, as well, but they're dealing with a corruption scandal, so who knows how many they can spare."

Emma forced a smile of acknowledgment, remembering the case she and Leo had helped the Boston Bureau close almost two weeks ago. Even with the extra bodies, the situation in Salem was nothing like she'd ever seen.

The chief's shoulder radio crackled, and he stepped away to respond. Emma heard him murmur something, but couldn't make out what he said. She exchanged glances with Mia and Leo.

Chief Peterson headed back their way, shaking his head. "Hey, if you want to help, we're getting reports of an explosion in a neighborhood near here."

Leo stepped forward, sweeping his arm wide, as if offering all three of them up as volunteers. "Where can we be the most help?"

"Detective Foss should have a team a few blocks over, right around her place. Link up with her."

With that, the chief headed back to his cruiser, got in, and roared off with his lights and sirens going full tilt.

Emma huddled close with her fellow agents. "If Celeste is the one causing the trouble, being right by her side to catch her in the act might be our best bet."

Leo held up his finger. "Or it could confirm that she's innocent, and Monique is the one we should be focused on."

As much as she hated to admit it, Emma couldn't deny his point. "Right. We still don't know which of them is our ally, if either one is. We have a lot of questions and not much else."

Mia nudged Emma. "Let's connect with Celeste and see how many answers we can get."

16

The streets leading to Celeste's home were littered with fires. Instead of sheltering as ordered, neighbors wandered the streets with their cell phones raised in front of them, recording it all.

Although Emma hadn't lived in the city for years, the sight of her hometown's destruction pained her. What began as a thimble-sized ball of nerves in her stomach had grown to a fist-sized weight of anger by the time they reached Celeste's address. "Wonder if she's home."

"Why would she be inside with all this going on?" Mia waved her arms in every direction.

"She didn't come out to help the sales guy when Brittany Weir attacked him."

"Couldn't we call her? She gave us her card." Leo jerked his chin, an impatient glare darkening his face.

Mia called, putting her phone on speaker. It went to voicemail.

Leo motioned at the house. "Lead on, Emma."

At the front porch, her knock was met with silence.

Leo stepped up beside Emma and had raised his fist for a

second knock when unmistakable gunshots rang out from inside the home.

"There's our exigent circumstance!" Leo drew his weapon and twisted the handle without waiting for her to agree. Emma and Mia drew their guns and flooded inside behind Leo as he announced their presence. "FBI! Put your weapons down and come out with your hands in clear view!"

His shout gained no more of a response than Emma's knock had.

The split-level home had a circular layout on the main floor. A small living area sat to the left, with doorways leading beyond it to what she already saw was a kitchen. Along the wall to their right, a staircase shot upward at a steep angle, but there was no movement to be seen anywhere.

Emma swept around the living room, with Mia and Leo covering her movement and monitoring the staircase and the doorway leading to the kitchen. With the living room cleared, Leo kept an eye on their six and the front entrance while Mia and Emma moved into the dining room, and finally the kitchen. "Main floor clear!"

Mia led the way down into the basement, Emma stacked behind her as Leo stayed on the ground floor. The space smelled dank and was packed with cardboard boxes, most of them covered in dust. Emma moved through and around them, searching where Celeste might be hiding, but they'd soon cleared the whole area and were heading back upstairs.

With Leo on point, the three agents stacked on the main floor steps, moving upstairs, continually calling out their presence and for anyone inside to drop their weapons and come out.

"FBI." Leo called out as they reached the top landing. "Come out with your hands up."

The house remained as silent and still as it had been when they first entered.

As a team, they moved room by room, still searching for Celeste or the source of the gunshots. In the first bedroom, located directly above the front door, they found a shotgun pointed at the ceiling, a hole directly above it. Emma gestured for Mia to guard the door while she and Leo stepped inside to examine the odd assembly. The weapon had been jerry-rigged with thick twine.

Emma put an arm out, making doubly sure that Leo didn't go any closer to the rig than necessary. "It went off when we knocked. We activated something."

"I don't like this." He gestured around the bedroom. It was reminiscent of a teenage girl's, with a corkboard, a bright-pink bedspread, and a canopy. But the dust showed that no one had lived here for a while.

Does Celeste have a kid? After giving my mother such crap?

But she only had Monique's word that Celeste was without family or friends. She hadn't thought to ask the detective.

"We need to finish clearing the house." Emma backed out of the room.

They passed the master bedroom. Celeste's bed was neatly made. Khaki bedclothes and furniture. It looked more like a sparsely furnished man cave than something that might belong to a woman as beautiful and put-together as Celeste.

Emma's throat tightened when they came to the final door, which housed a staircase to the attic. "Looks like we go up. Mia, you okay staying here to keep an eye out?"

Mia gestured them upward and turned to face the hallway again, just in case Celeste came home. They were close to having the house cleared, but that didn't mean someone wouldn't attempt to sneak up on them from behind if given the chance.

Emma took point this time but found herself having to force each step forward as she moved up and into the dim space. Inside the room, she gripped a cord attached to a bare bulb and pulled.

It was a traditional attic. The space was clean and organized. Bookshelves lined one low wall.

Leo bent in front of a stack of journals, pointing to a loose pile of papers beside them. "Lots of writing in some other language. I don't recognize it."

Before she could respond, the air went cold and thick, and Emma whirled around the center of the room with her flashlight raised.

Oren.

She got a brief glance of his wild dark hair and panicked expression before he rushed toward her and Leo, waving his arms and screaming. "Get out! Get out!"

His panic infected the air, choking off Emma's breath. The last time he'd warned her of impending disaster, a bomb had knocked their colleague Vance Jessup out of commission. He'd been lucky to live.

Emma didn't think. She stuffed her gun back into her holster and grabbed Leo's arm before she lost whatever time they had left.

"Leo, we have to—"

An explosion rocked the home, and Emma fell forward into her partner as Mia screamed from below.

Leo grunted beneath her, and Emma rolled sideways toward the staircase. There was no time to collect Celeste's papers. Leo crawled after her as Mia's head poked above the line of the floorboard.

"Go, Mia! We're right behind you!"

Smoke burned Emma's throat and eyes, the attic already foggy with it, but she stumbled down the stairs with Leo at her back.

Farther down the second-floor hallway, Mia stood outlined by flames moving up the walls of the first-floor staircase. She turned to them with one hand over her mouth. "It's coming from the kitchen too! The stairs are out!"

She collapsed forward in a cough. Emma hurried forward and grabbed her arms, pulling her backward alongside Leo. The flames were faster, though, surrounding them. Fire burst in through the bedroom windows from the outside. They stumbled back down the hall and into the bathroom, which faced the backyard.

Leo slammed the bathroom door shut behind them. Smoke was already crawling into the space, and Mia crouched, coughing into her sleeve as Emma opened the window. Flames licked up the exterior siding of the back of the house too. But they had a better chance of survival here than jumping onto the cement and rock-covered ground in the front yard. At least the back had a natural slope. The homes had been built into a hill, and the fall was shorter.

Flames shot into the air from below them, hotter than anything in Emma's memory. At the same time, smoke poured beneath the door.

Sirens had begun sounding from somewhere, but there wasn't any time to wait.

Mia leaped, coughing as she did, and flew over the flames, landing on the grass behind the house and rolling as she hit the ground. Emma perched on the sill and, after a glance backward to ensure Leo was ready to follow, she gathered herself and took a deep breath. The heat of the flames felt like it might melt her boots as she pushed off the sill and leaped for all she was worth.

The fire was beneath her and then behind her. The ground raked the air from her lungs as she landed and rolled, her whole body jarred by the impact. She came to a stop just short of hitting a tree. Mia, already on her feet, helped her to sit up. A loud grunt signaled Leo's landing nearby.

When she found her breath, she ran her hands along her legs and arms to feel for any injuries. The grassy lawn had cushioned the fall, and nothing was broken. She glanced over to Leo, who winced as he stood up beside Mia. Their faces were smudged with soot, but neither appeared hurt.

Another bang sounded from the house, and they flinched backward as one.

When Emma looked up again, the whole second floor of Celeste's house had been engulfed in flames.

But more than that, she knew something else. That fire had been meant to kill them.

17

With Emma in the lead, the three of them pushed through a haze of smoke and cinders along the side yard and reached the front sidewalk, where they all doubled over coughing amid shouts and screams from people rushing around the area.

Emma feebly reached for her weapon, fearing an attack. But when she finally stood and looked around, she was met with a scene of utter chaos and destruction.

Flames roared from Celeste's home, blanketing the immediate area in thick smoke. Even worse, the fire had spread to neighboring homes. Smoke clouded the air. It looked as if the whole suburb would be ablaze in minutes.

Leo choked on the sooty air growing heavier around them. "I didn't smell gas beforehand. Some kind of bomb?"

"Has to be. But did she do it to her own house? Or did Monique do this?"

Another home down the block erupted in an explosion of flames and smoke, followed by a third, and then two others on the opposite side of the street.

The roar of the fires was deafening. Leo slapped a hand

on her shoulder, pulling her into the street. Mia had already begun running for their Malibu but changed course to keep up with them.

Around them, shouts and sirens disturbed the air on every side, but a high-pitched scream, overpowering it all, drew Emma's eyes.

Across the street, Brittany Weir chased her husband, Trevor, outside the house. It hadn't caught fire—not yet, at least—but Brittany's white eyes all but glowed in the smoky air as her husband screamed in terror. He tripped, falling on his face, and Emma took off at a sprint.

She reached the woman with Leo and Mia right behind her. Brittany raised a knife high, ready to strike. Emma batted her arm aside and tackled her to the ground. Just as she got Brittany's hand twisted above her head, Leo grabbed the knife from it and helped control the flailing woman.

Her husband pleaded with them from where he sat on their lawn. "Look at her eyes! That's not her. She needs a doctor. Don't hurt her, please!"

Emma glanced over. "We're not going to hurt her, Mr. Weir."

Her heart wrenched open as he nodded, more tears streaming down his face as he watched Leo cuff his wife.

"We're going to leave her in your custody until we can get someone out here to help."

Trevor nodded, eyes still on his wife. "Th-thank you."

Mia's lips pinched together, biting back what might've been a sob, as she led Trevor up to his front porch. Emma and Leo maneuvered the still-screaming Brittany up after them.

As incredible as it was, it seemed like they were in the middle of a zombie movie. Worse, they kind of where, but these zombies had an evil puppet master pulling their strings.

When they'd gotten Brittany pushed down to the floor inside the front door, Leo handed the knife off to Trevor, and they headed back outside, pausing on the sidewalk to check for messages from Jacinda.

"Nothing yet. She must be on the road or in the air."

"Agents," Trevor called to them from the porch, "she's herself again, but…we're going to keep her in cuffs just in case. For now."

Brittany stood beside her husband, her brown pupils back in place. "Please…find out what's going on. Help us." Her voice shook with terror.

Leo held up his keys. "Are you sure you want to stay cuffed?"

"No, leave them on. He says I tried to kill him." Brittany choked on the words.

Emma reached for Leo's shoulder, pulling him back up. "We'll come back when we can. And we'll send help."

For whatever good it will do.

Back at the car, they all climbed in. Emma tried Celeste's phone this time as Leo got the engine started. "Any luck?"

"No answer. It keeps going straight to voicemail."

He maneuvered them around burning cars and fleeing pedestrians. Their crazy-looking vehicle fit right in with all the destruction.

The whole city seemed to be in chaos.

Leo took a hard left at a blocked intersection, and their GPS updated their route. Emma kept silent as he concentrated on driving.

When they finally reached the police station, Leo rolled to a stop on the side of the road, leaving them to stare at the scene before them.

The building was engulfed in flames. A line of people stood in the street filming the destruction.

World War Z come to life.

Leo's knuckles were white as he clutched the steering wheel. "We have to do something. We can't just sit here."

"What are we gonna do?" Emma bit her lip hard enough to taste blood. "It's too late to save the station or anyone inside. And nobody's in charge here. Might be time to call in the National Guard."

Mia gripped Emma's hand tight. "There's no guarantee they wouldn't succumb to the same madness we're seeing here. How is this even happening? Do ghosts…these Shade things…can they just possess someone like that?"

Emma paused before answering, searching her memory for anything that might help explain what they were dealing with. Her meetings with Marigold, her psychic friend and mentor, had never touched directly on the idea of possession.

But both Monique and Celeste could be capable of manipulating innocent people through the Other. Emma had never encountered a ghost who wanted to possess or control someone still alive, though.

You kinda know what it's like to be possessed, though, thanks to Monique. She used a ghost to pull you into the Other against your will.

"These things aren't usually malevolent on their own. Not the ones I've seen anyway. They mostly want to communicate a message, if anything. Unless someone else is controlling them."

Mia drummed the fingers of her free hand on the shoulder of Leo's seat. "We can't fight this with badges and guns, even if we had an endless supply. Whatever's behind all this, it doesn't obey the laws of physics, or any laws, for that matter. We have to stop this at its source."

Leo turned the car back on and shifted into reverse. "What we need to do is find a safe place to concentrate and figure out our next steps."

Bending forward, Emma fished her phone from where it had fallen beneath the seat and turned the police scanner app on. Outside the vehicle, Shades lined the road as Leo maneuvered between two smashed cars that blocked most of the road.

An adolescent spirit stalked around in front of them, waving translucent arms dripping blood.

Emma bent her head, blocking out the carnage and focusing on her phone. She'd never seen ghosts so willfully acting out for her, as if her attention alone were all that mattered.

Could that mean that whichever woman was manipulating the ghosts to do her bidding was also watching Emma through their eyes.

Trust Celeste or trust Monique?

I just don't know, dammit!

"Keep going, Leo. Just get us out of this. And then we'll figure out how to stop it all."

Her stomach twisted as they left the spirits behind.

She hadn't said what she wanted to say.

That it might already be too late to stop it.

18

With Leo driving them out of the city center and away from the bulk of the chaos, Emma brought up a map on her tablet and browsed local news sites on her tablet. She didn't know quite what she was looking for.

Leo pulled into an empty elementary school parking lot and turned off the engine.

Reaching over, Mia pointed to a map on Emma had loaded up on her tablet. "There's another fire near the police station. And two by city hall."

Emma marked the locations with red dots. They spent several minutes tagging locations. The map of Salem was a sea of red. Every street through the city center had multiple hot spots flagged, and a mass of red dots filled Salem's western boundary.

"It looks like the whole city is about to be on fire."

Mia offered a groan of commiseration. "I tried Celeste's phone again. Still no answer, and there's no way to tell where she might be based on this."

"What do you mean 'this?'"

"I mean I'm trying to geo profile on whoever's behind this. Her house is at the center, from what I'm seeing."

Emma's hackles went up. "That could mean she's the instigator."

"Can we stop assuming the worst about her?" Leo slapped the steering wheel. "Sure, her house being at the center might mean she's 'the instigator,' but it could also mean that's where the real perpetrator started their campaign of terror and violence to make Celeste look guilty."

"I have to agree, Emma." Mia pressed her lips together. "Her house being at the epicenter doesn't tell us for certain that she's behind everything."

Emma drooped back against the seat. "And we know she's not there."

"Exactly." Leo pounded the wheel again. Leaning over to tap Emma's tablet, he zoomed out the city view.

At first, the screen still showed a sea of red, but as the dots blurred together, a picture began to take shape. "Shit, Leo, you're a genius. Talk about signs."

Loose as the image was, there was no denying the shape that emerged from the dots. *An arrow.*

Leo snorted. "Probably another trap."

"Do we have a choice?" Emma tried to ignore the resistance dripping from Leo's tone. She carefully zoomed in on the image.

Remaining quiet, Leo and Mia both watched as Emma brought them closer and closer to the very point of the arrow. At a level where the exact streets were visible, the arrow pointed past a neighborhood and out to the city limits.

"It leads to a spot near Monique's cabin. Maybe their Place of Moonlight? Monique said it was nearby."

Leo jabbed his finger at the tablet screen. "This doesn't mean Celeste can't be our guilty party, but I'd say we've been thinking too hard about the wrong person." He pushed the button to start the engine and wheeled them out of the parking lot. "I'll go back to the same place we parked on our first trip to Monique's. We should be able to walk it from there."

Emma twisted to look at him. "You sound convinced Monique is the villain. Care to elaborate?"

Leo drove in silence, his face stony as he kept his focus on the road. They exited the neighborhoods and were back on the road toward Monique's hideaway in the preserve.

Emma doubled down on her question. "No reply, Leo? Have you considered that Celeste is framing Monique?"

He barked a laugh. "Sure. Celeste wants us to look at Monique, so she burns her own house down. That tracks."

Mia gave a hum of reluctant agreement. "That is a lot of sacrifice for one person. If you think about it, she's lost her station, her coworkers, and her home all in one day. Her neighborhood's on fire as we speak."

"The obvious answer is that we consider Monique the perpetrator, since the arrow's taking us in her direction." Leo touched the gas a smidge harder, sending them speeding through an intersection abutting a large construction site.

Emma's stomach turned, and it wasn't due to the increase in ghosts wandering about. Leo and Mia had willingly joined her on this trip. What began as a mission had become a nightmare.

And now we're more divided than we've ever been. Even if we do figure out who's behind all of this, what hope do we have of stopping them?

After more than a dozen harrowing moments, with speeding cars cutting them off and detours around damaged roadways, they were on the roads leading to the wetland preserve around Monique's property.

The road, thankfully, was empty of other traffic. But the track was still heavily rutted and full of twists and turns.

They eventually reached their parking spot outside Monique's gate, and Leo cut the engine.

As they climbed out of the vehicle, an unmarked police car came around the last turn. Through the windshield, Detective Celeste Foss was clearly visible. She pulled the car to a sudden halt, nearly tapping her front bumper against the Malibu's rear end.

"Shit." Leo's eyes widened with surprise. "Where'd she come from? I didn't see anyone tailing me."

From behind the wheel of the cruiser, Celeste Foss's face was bright pink with fury. The older woman practically threw herself out of the car and stalked up to the trio. Her hands were fisted and trembling. Strands of silvery hair caught in a breeze and whipped around her head like snakes.

Her eyes, bloodshot with either rage or fatigue, zeroed in on Emma, who half expected the cop to throw a punch, but Celeste managed to hold it together enough to speak through bared teeth.

"What the hell happened to my house? My neighborhood?"

Mia stepped forward, flashing her dimples in a comforting yet professional smile. "We're trying to figure that out, Detective Foss. Why don't you head back into Salem and—"

"Oh, I don't think so, Agent Logan." Celeste mirrored Mia's professional tone and use of title rather than given name. "Whatever you're investigating, I'm going with you. And if Monique is at the end of it, I'm arresting her."

She can't arrest anyone for using magic any more than we can.

Celeste turned on Emma before anyone could respond. "And I don't need your permission, my girl. This is my jurisdiction. One call, and I can have you all pulled back to D.C., stating that you're being uncooperative with our office."

Emma gritted her teeth. Jacinda *probably* wouldn't pull them back on the emotional request of a stressed-out local detective, especially given backup was on their way. She tried to redirect. "We've been trying to contact you all morning. Where've you been?"

Celeste blinked at her. "Where have I been? Have you seen Salem right now? I was just involved in a shoot-out with an axe-wielding maniac. Damien Knight? Remember him? I've been *busy*."

"Considering Salem's situation, I think you should probably focus on—"

"Hold it right there, my girl. This is *my* town being burned. *My* house that was destroyed." She stamped her foot. "If you think I'm leaving without confronting the real threat to Salem, you are dead wrong."

Fuck.

"Fine."

"What?" Mia stared at Emma like she'd grown two heads.

Emma ignored her and directed her instructions to Celeste. "You can come with us. You know these parts better than we do. But put one toe out of line, try to hurt Monique, and I will shoot you. I mean it." As soon as the words left her mouth, Emma realized she really did mean it.

Celeste seemed to sense Emma's sincerity. She stood down, her shoulders relaxing and her color returning to her normal level of pale. "Fine."

"You stick with Agent Ambrose. Leo, keep an eye on her."

He nodded but didn't meet Emma's gaze. "Lead the way."

Emma moved forward with Mia just behind her.

A deep Other chill washed over Emma's shoulders from behind, as if impelling her or pulling her forward. "Let's go. I'm either being pushed or pulled through the Other. We'll follow the cold where it takes us."

Leo fell in line with Celeste behind Mia. "Are you sure

following the cold is safe? What if you end up leading us right into a trap?"

"Keep your eyes open, just like we did in Buckskin."

"I'm pretty sure I know where we're going." Celeste matched Leo's pace.

Emma ignored her bravado. Together, they made their way over the marshy ground and around the rusty green gate that separated the road to Monique's cabin from the public area of the wilderness preserve.

Despite fearing an attack that might freeze her in place, leaving her friends burdened and in danger, she kept trekking toward the chill. The Other cold led them away from the road they'd taken the other day. Pushing aside low-hanging branches, Emma forged ahead and found herself on a hidden trail through the woods.

Behind her, Celeste whistled low. "I knew it. Told you. We're going to the Place of Moonlight."

"How do you know?" Emma threw a quick look over her shoulder to see Celeste holding a branch out of the way for Leo.

"Because I'm not an idiot, my girl." She met Emma's gaze and smiled. "Gina and I used a different route from the other side of the preserve. There're a dozen trails that can get there, but where else would we be going?"

Emma continued moving, pushing against the cold that grew denser and stronger the more she walked. She turned, moving around a rotted tree, and came to a dead end.

"This way." Celeste's voice came through the trees, and Emma backtracked to find her pointing out a path Emma hadn't seen.

"This path looks purposefully cut, which makes me think it's a trap." Leo stopped walking. "Emma, can we talk about this?"

Celeste stepped forward on the trail. "Monique used to

come out here and build switchbacks and dead ends, in case anyone ever found her secret. That's why this is purposefully cut. It's also probably a trap."

The woman's mild confirmation irked Emma. She had a reply on her tongue, but a long smear of crimson on the ground caught her eye. She jerked her head up, scanning the area.

Ahead on the trail, the ghost of Brittany Weir swayed from side to side. Emma's gut twisted. An enormous gash down her torso spilled viscera and blood in a translucent cascade.

"What is it, Emma?" Mia's question was quickly echoed by Leo.

Before Emma could form a reply, Celeste answered for her. "There's a Shade in front of us. Brittany Weir, formerly my neighbor across the street. She's been cut open."

Leo let out a string of curses. "You're kidding. She was fine not that long ago."

Had they made a mistake leaving her handcuffed with her husband free? Had Trevor fallen under the influence, taken the knife, and killed his helpless wife?

Anything could've happened in the time since Brittany had begged them to leave her cuffed, but Emma hoped she was wrong.

"You can see the ghosts too?" Mia sounded incredulous. She looked at Emma for confirmation. "Is she telling the truth?"

Emma nodded as she moved between branches, being careful not to step into the smears of blood on the ground. Mia came up behind her.

She glanced at Brittany's ghost once more, hoping the spirit would offer some clue or hint at least, but the Shade merely moaned and wandered deeper into the woods.

Leo joined them and fired questions at Celeste as she let

some branches fall back into place. "Can you ask the ghost what's going on? Maybe get an idea of what we're walking into here?"

The cop in Celeste emerged. Her hands came out of her pockets to rest on her belt, thumbs tucked in. "Even if I did ask them, who knows what they'd offer as a reply? Unless Emma's figured out how to decipher Shade babble, we're better off ignoring them."

"Have they always been this unhelpful?" Emma asked her.

Celeste nodded. "For those of us who know better than to try controlling them. The longer we stand here, the more time Monique has to do just that."

Around Emma, more Shades flickered in and out of the trees. She studied Celeste's haggard face for a moment before turning away. "Guess we should keep going, then." She marched onward, following Brittany's trail, the cold of the Other biting into her with each step.

Is Celeste freezing too? She doesn't look it.

When Emma picked up her pace, Mia jogged to keep up with her. "You're shivering, and we're not seeing anything that looks like a circle of moonlight."

"It's daytime." Celeste's voice rang out from the back of the line.

"Are you sure this is the right direction?"

Emma didn't respond but put a hand on her gun, ready to draw if need be. "Everyone, keep an eye out. This blood is fresh." She pointed to a branch.

A woman's bloody ghost stumbled across the path ahead, but she was too far away for Emma to determine whether it was still Brittany or someone else.

"She can see you!" The ghost let out a scream and ran off into the trees.

For Emma, the words pierced her sharper than a knife's point. That was what her mother had yelled at her once from the Other. The only time she'd heard her mother's voice since she was tiny. She whirled to face Celeste.

The detective held her hands up in mock surrender. "Caught!" She rolled her eyes. "Of course I can see you. I'm looking right at you."

Mia looked from Emma to Celeste. "What's she talking about?"

"Ghosts." It was the only answer she could give. She came to a slow halt and took a break to rub her hands over her arms, attempting to brush away the goose bumps.

"Is it really not as bad as it was before?" Leo came up to just behind her, speaking flatly, robotically. "Or are you pretending for our sakes?"

Once again, Celeste answered first. "She's pretending."

"Enough from the peanut gallery!" Emma whirled on Celeste, ready to send her back to the cars.

Mia nudged Emma with an elbow and turned to Leo, studying him. "You okay? You sound…off."

"I'm fine." Leo's "resting face" always came with a slight smile, but his thin-lipped expression now appeared to have flat-lined, just like his voice sounded. He squinted at them. "What are we doing? Forward or not?" He looked past Emma's shoulder, as if to force the point.

"Monique could be tricking us."

"You think?" Sarcasm dripped from Celeste's words.

Emma hugged herself, trying to put aside Leo's odd behavior and Celeste's aggressive and mocking attitude. She needed to think.

Mia swiped one hand across her forehead, brushing away some beads of sweat. "Could she have faked that letter from your mom?"

Emma peered around the woods as if they might hold the answer to the question. "I don't know. I didn't think so yesterday, but…I don't know."

"I know." Celeste watched each of them. "She blew up my damn house. She's left a trail of destruction for us, well, for *you* to follow, on a path that she liked to claim as her own. This is all clearly a setup, and I'm walking into it with you. Do you still think I'm the better suspect?"

Leo sighed. "I have doubts. We should go to Monique's and quiz her and Celeste together."

Emma took another glance at Leo. In the shadow of the trees, his eyes looked dimmer than usual.

She faced the woods again, mind made up. "We keep going."

19

Another ghost appeared off to the left, this one unmistakably familiar. Emma came to a halt as Officer Sandra Vales staggered in her direction, clutching at a deep gash running down her torso.

Mia stepped in beside her. "What is it, Emma? Why'd you stop?"

"It's Officer Vales. She's dead too."

"Another cop from my station." Celeste's growl cut through the forest around them. "That makes three of my people dead because of Monique."

"Gotta keep going." Emma quietly muttered words of encouragement to herself, dreading what awaited them at the Place of Moonlight.

"We're close, Emma. I know it." Leo surprised her by speaking directly into her ear.

She startled and jumped, almost colliding with Mia.

"What is it?"

"I don't know. I thought…" She looked back at Leo, who was at least twenty feet back.

Celeste looked at her with her eyebrows raised. "Can we get going? The sooner, the better."

Another ghost, this one also a woman, began pacing off to the right. Emma couldn't identify her through the trees, but the figure was lifting her arms as if to point Emma at the path ahead.

Monique had said something about the Place of Moonlight being a power center for her, Emma's mother, and Celeste. If they were being led into a trap, she hoped Celeste really was on their side.

Having followed a slight bend around a huge holly bush, they entered a large clearing ringed by trees in a near perfect circle.

This has to be the Place of Moonlight.

Emma stumbled to a halt and looked for Celeste, wanting to gauge the woman's reaction to seeing the space.

Several paces back from where Emma stood, Leo was propping himself up with one hand against a tree trunk. The other clutched his shin, as if he'd banged his leg against something.

Celeste had her hand on his shoulder to steady him.

Emma watched the woman closely. "Everything okay, Leo? Celeste?"

She waved a hand in Emma's direction. "All good. He just barked his shin."

"I'm fine." Leo lifted his hand away from the tree trunk and jumped back. "What the…" Blood smeared across his palm and dripped from his fingers.

"It's not yours. Come on." Celeste led him away from the tree.

He rubbed the blood on his jeans. "It's all over the tree."

"It's not just on the tree." Celeste pointed into the clearing. "Look. We found Brittany Weir and Sandra Vales. Who's that with them?"

Emma stepped toward the center of the circle with Mia on her heels.

Three women were lying with their heads together. Each woman's hands were clasped to the others' beside her, forming a ring.

The women's chests had been sliced open, and blood trailed out and soaked into the ground, turning the grass around the bodies into spikes of red. Flies swarmed.

These women had been killed during the chaos of Salem's fires. One of them was a cop.

But Brittany and Officer Vales were fine when we last saw them.

Sandra Vales was in the middle of the rioting, but Chief Peterson was with her. Brittany had recently been possessed again but had come out of her stupor. They'd left her handcuffed and under the watchful eye of her husband, Trevor.

Moving closer, Emma thought she recognized the third victim by the apron she had on, though she'd also been sliced open and was mostly covered in blood.

Emma's stomach dropped. Mary Evert.

"Where's Luca?"

"Who?" Leo's disgusted tone sent Emma spinning around to confront him.

"The baby! Mary Evert had an infant in her arms when we spoke with her yesterday." Emma pushed her hand through her hair. "Where is he?"

Celeste stepped forward, placing a hand on Leo's shoulder and drawing him back from Emma. "Chief Peterson and I heard reports of missing children this morning. It's just one of the crises plaguing the city right now. I don't know if Luca Evert was among those reported, but as soon as we're done here, I'll find out." She looked around. "Where the hell is Monique?"

Emma ignored her. She'd thought Monique would be here, too, but the message was received. *These three poor dead women.*

"They're holding hands." Mia had her phone out and began taking photos and geotagging. "This blood's pretty fresh."

Emma held a hand to her brow. "We spoke to Brittany Weir, alive, less than two hours ago. Office Vales too. These are all recent murders. Someone had to have just killed them. Look at all the blood."

"All for one. One for all." Celeste snarled. "That bitch. That unbelievably self-righteous *bitch*." The violence in her voice was as chilling as the Other. A strange wind swirled around her. With the wind came a distant, familiar howl, and more tendrils of Celeste's silvery hair pulled loose from her French twist.

"What is it, Celeste?" Emma faced the woman. The energy pouring off her mother's friend hit her in waves, alternating her skin between hot and cold.

"We used to come here and look at the stars. Me, Monique, and your mother. We'd lie down and hold hands just like that. She killed my witness, my colleague, and my neighbor to bastardize our friendship." Celeste stepped right up to Emma, almost nose to nose. "Enough. I've indulged your little investigation too long. I know who's responsible. We go talk to Monique right now."

Energy seemed to surge through Leo as well. His eyes opened wide, and a half smile curled his lips. "Couldn't agree with her more, Emma. It's time to go see Monique."

Emma tilted her head, examining his face and eyes. Something was off, and she couldn't quite put her finger on it.

He looks like Leo, and mostly talks like Leo. But...

"You good?"

"Am I good? You seeing this?" He gestured at the dead women. "Who wouldn't be a little freaked out? But we have a strong lead, and the *Trust Monique* column is about as empty as can be. Let's *go*."

Everything he said was true.

And yet, somehow, Emma was not convinced.

She looked back and forth from Leo to Mia. "Maybe we should all regroup. We need to alert Chief Peterson about this. One of his officers is dead. Murdered. Forensics needs to—"

"Seriously?" Leo glared at her, upper lip curled in a sneer. "You can't just trust the *detective* standing next to me, who's lived here all her life? You need the chief's approval? I'm trying to rationalize what I'm hearing with the knowledge that you're the same person who has, several times, lit out after a suspect despite being *ordered* to stand down and wait."

Emma had no answer to his diatribe. He wasn't acting like himself, not by a long shot, but he wasn't wrong either. "Okay. You win. Lead the way, and let's see what Monique has to say for herself."

Celeste put a calming hand on Leo's shoulder. "Emma has a point, Leo, but I appreciate the solidarity. Let's get going."

Emma watched them turn and depart, like partners who'd worked together for years. She swallowed down the anger that had risen in her throat, meeting Mia's worried gaze before she could make her feet move.

Leo isn't remotely fine. Not by any definition of the word.

But no matter how he'd just snapped at her, she had to hope their partnership would be strong enough to see them through whatever came next.

20

Leo traipsed beside Celeste, following the path without really seeing where his feet were landing. He let them lead the way, wanting to take time and ensure his emotions cooled.

Why had he snapped at Emma like that anyway? It was like his mouth had a mind of its own.

Glancing down, he saw the remnants of the blood from that tree on his palm. For the second time in as many minutes, he wiped his palm on his jeans. The blood had dried into the cracks and creases in his skin.

If he'd had water, he would've washed his hands. He almost spit on his palm but couldn't bring himself to do it.

You've had blood on your hands before.

Suddenly, he was swamped with memories of holding Denae's lifeless form, performing CPR compressions to keep her alive, and watching her blood seep through her shirt, coating his hands.

At the hospital that day, with the EMTs racing away from him with Denae on a gurney, he'd collapsed into a chair. Her blood stained his hands and clothes, but he refused to wash it off, as if removing the only traces of her he could hold on to would mean losing her forever.

Jacinda had brought over a packet of sanitary wipes and tried to clean his hands for him.

You jerked away and screamed at her. She was trying to take Denae away from you.

His rational mind knew that wasn't true, but in the moment, he'd only known one thing about the blood on his hands.

"The blood was there because you weren't able to protect her." Celeste's voice murmured in his ear.

"What?" He turned to face her, challenging. But she wasn't beside him. She was a good ten feet back.

"You couldn't save her." This time, Celeste's voice came from the opposite side. "She almost died. She's better off without you. Safer."

He spun in the other direction. No Celeste. He stopped and did a one-eighty. Celeste was walking up to meet him, a questioning look on her face. There was no way she could've whispered right into his ear. It sounded like her voice was coming from inside his head—it felt that close to him.

"You okay, Leo?"

He merely swallowed and turned back around.

The strange shadows from his experience in the woods yesterday began to take shape as he plowed forward.

Emma and Mia paced them, chatting as if the world wasn't about to end. Mia pointed at a tree. He followed her finger to where a gray bird had alighted before pecking at some bark and taking flight once more.

Emma reminded Mia they needed to stay alert. "I'm seeing a lot of ghosts now, wandering all around us, and they do not look friendly."

A chill ran down Leo's spine. He spotted movement

shifting through the trees too. Ghosts. They had to be. But why could he see them?

He touched a tree as he passed it without thinking, and it seemed to tremble. The fog clouding his thoughts grew thicker, blurring his vision now. Emma and Mia were getting too far ahead.

"These Shades aren't happy to see us." Celeste fell into step with him.

Why did she say that? Did she know that he was seeing them now too?

The path ahead bent, and Emma and Mia were about to turn with it, taking them around a thick stand of trees where he wouldn't be able to see them. The idea of being left behind with Celeste was terrifying.

He was ready to cry out for them to slow down when the fog lifted and his eyes cleared.

What the hell? Was it just extreme stress?

Leo shook away the confusion and hurried away from Celeste to catch up.

Emma glanced back as he got closer. "You okay there, Leo?"

A grin crept across his face, full and assured. "Absolutely. Lead the way."

She hesitated but then did as he instructed.

That was good. The last thing he wanted was for them to see any sign of the confusion, fear, and rage bubbling in his gut.

21

Monique's cabin finally came into view, and Emma exhaled a long breath. She spotted her weathered truck sitting right where it had been parked before. If Emma had to guess, she would say the truck hadn't moved in a few days, certainly not since her last visit to the cabin.

Ever since they'd found that clearing, she'd felt as if they'd stepped on a land mine—similar to the way she'd felt walking through the Virginia woods, narrowly avoiding trip wires— but the sight of Monique's cabin, visible through the trees, brought nothing short of relief, even though they were there to confront her.

"Finally." Celeste stepped forward, looking prepared to charge the front door.

"Whoa, whoa." Emma moved in front of her. "Not you. You bring heat to an already red-hot situation. Mia and I can handle Monique."

Celeste's brown eyes widened. "Did you see what I saw in that clearing? You think you can *handle* her, my girl?"

Don't trust Celeste. You don't know enough.

"If we need help, we'll call you and Leo." She turned to

Leo, who looked oddly pale but otherwise okay. "Stay here with Celeste. We'll call if we need you."

He gave her a nod and turned to stare toward Monique's cabin. "Go ahead. We'll wait for your word."

Emma and Mia continued past the edge of the woods and approached the cabin. Little as she knew about Monique and her potential powers, Emma doubted wandering up to her door unannounced was a good idea. She stopped with Mia a safe distance away.

A vision of the three dead women in the clearing shot through her brain. She had a hard time imagining Monique doing such a horrid thing.

"Monique, are you here?" Emma called out, moving toward the cabin. When she got no answer, she raised her voice a touch. "It's Emma and Mia! We have some more questions!"

Monique came out the door, wiping her hands on an apron smeared with red, a slight frown to her face. "I didn't expect you back so soon. Is everything okay?"

"We found a clearing about a mile to the east."

"The Place of Moonlight." It wasn't a question.

"Have you been there recently, earlier today, maybe?"

Shaking her head, Monique stepped onto her porch. "I hardly go there anymore, not since Gina...we always went there at night, anyway, not during the day. Stargazing was one of our ways of spending quiet moments together."

Lying down and looking at the stars. Three friends holding hands.

"So that's where you, Mom, and Celeste gathered?"

"It was, yes, but I'm the only one who's been there in years. Why would you go there?"

If you're "the only one who's been there in years," you might have just confessed to a triple homicide.

"We were following a lead. And we found three women. Murdered. Lying head-to-head, holding hands."

The older woman paled. Emma lowered her gaze from Monique's face to the red stains on her apron. As far as she could tell, the woman had been working with some kind of fruit, maybe making preserves.

That's not blood, but that doesn't mean she didn't possess someone else and force them to kill those women.

"Can you account for your whereabouts this morning, from about five thirty onward?"

According to Celeste, Monique didn't have to leave her cabin to wreak havoc, but starting out with an alibi for that time frame seemed right.

Monique gripped the post of her front porch. When she spoke, her voice barely managed a trace of the confidence she possessed before. "You're…you suspect me of murder?"

Mia stepped forward. "We're just following procedure. Where were you between the hours of five thirty and nine thirty this morning?"

"I was here. Making strawberry jam." She gestured at her stained apron. "Are you sure this isn't all an elaborate ruse Celeste built to distract you?"

"We took pictures, for evidence." Mia held up her phone screen for the woman. "In case that isn't clear."

Normally, Emma wouldn't condone handing raw photos to a potential suspect. But these were not normal times. They needed to get a rise out of Monique if they could.

"Oh, no. Oh, no. Oh, no." All the blood drained from Monique's face. "She's killed more people. She desecrated our clearing."

Emma opened her mouth to ask more questions, but a figure slammed into her, sending her sprawling. The attack came so fast, she hit the wood of the porch without bracing herself. Her head bashed onto a step, and pops of light exploded before her vision righted itself.

As the world came back into focus, she realized Mia was on the ground, too, equally stunned and perhaps a second or two behind Emma in getting her bearings.

But the sight that terrified her the most was Monique sprawled out, just inside her front door now, a dark figure on top of her.

It was Leo.

He was strangling Monique.

"Shit." She lunged forward up the steps of the porch, trying to get purchase as she leaped on Leo's back. "Leo, let go! Stand down, dammit!"

His shoulder muscles were taut, his arms locked, and he was leaning into Monique's throat with the entire weight of his body. He barely acknowledged Emma's presence on his back.

From the corner of her eye, Emma saw Mia jump over them, turn, and punch Leo straight in the face. It was a solid connection—Emma felt it as she tried to yank Leo off-balance. But he didn't flinch, either from Mia's punch or Emma's pulling.

Without thinking, Emma wrapped an arm around Leo's neck in a sleeper hold. She squeezed harder than she'd been trained to, but she had to stop him.

Monique was purple. Her eyes were already bloodshot from broken capillaries. They didn't have much time at all.

"His eyes are white, Emma!" Mia scrabbled to pull his fingers off Monique's throat, but she clearly couldn't get her fingers under his without adding more pressure.

For what must've been only a second, but which felt like an eternity, Emma thought they might have to shoot him to get him to stop. She didn't know if she could do it. So she squeezed tighter, holding on for dear life.

"Hit him again!" Emma hollered at Mia. "Vase!"

Mia understood Emma's staccato command. She grabbed a vase of violets and lavender, then swung with all her might.

The impact reverberated through both Leo and Emma. Water splashed everywhere as the vase shattered against Leo's temple. Tiny shards of glass cut her arms and forehead, but she'd closed her eyes to avoid any damage there.

Flowers were everywhere. Monique and Leo and Emma were drenched. And he was bleeding from the head.

Still, he held his grip.

Until, with a sudden shift, the tight muscles against Emma's chest and under her squeezing arms relaxed. They both collapsed on top of Monique. She groaned and coughed feebly, a rasping sound escaping her lips.

Emma rolled off, pulling Leo with her. "Mia, check Monique, please. I'll stay with Leo."

She slid him out of the way and laid him on his back. When she bent down to hold her ear over his mouth, the distinct heat of his breath was warm on her cheek. A small shot of relief relaxed her.

Before Mia could even reach Monique, the woman had crab-crawled backward and was sitting up. Her eyes were glassy, and the whites were a bright, veiny red. Another few moments of being strangled, and she wouldn't have been getting up. Bruises were already polka-dotting her throat. Emma had the weird thought that the bruising was the exact same color as the lavender and violets now scattered among them. The cloying scents made her want to gag.

The air was filled with the sound of everyone's breath.

After a deep inhale, Leo jolted awake. His eyes were his normal deep brown and full of confusion. "What the hell happened?"

"I could ask you the same thing." Emma helped him sit up.

A bloody bruise had formed where Mia had struck him with the vase, but otherwise, he seemed unharmed.

Monique seemed to know what happened, though. "Celeste. She got into his mind."

Celeste.

"Where is she?" Emma pushed herself up to her knees, looking out to the front yard. "You were with her, Leo."

Monique scrambled up to her knees. "You brought her *here*? To my home?"

"We didn't know if we could trust you *or* her." Mia moved to Emma and helped her stand. "Unfortunately, now we know we definitely can't trust her. And I'm guessing we have no idea where she's run off to."

Emma strode to the edge of the front porch. As Mia had said, there was no sign of the other woman. She'd been down the trail with Leo, probably using their alone time to fuck with his mind.

When she turned back to the cabin door, Leo was helping Monique stand. Apologies tumbled out of his mouth, his shoulders hunched in almost a bow. The anger that had flashed so briefly was gone now.

After a moment, Monique held her hand up. "Enough apologizing. You weren't yourself." Examining Leo's cuts, she grabbed a tube of ointment off her table. "Put this on."

As he dabbed the ointment onto his temple, Monique looked the three agents over. "So you believe me now? After you brought that…vile bitch to my home?"

Feeling like a scolded toddler, Emma nodded.

The Trust Monique *column…check, check, check, ding, ding, ding.*

"Celeste wanted to come here to try to kill me. If she kills me, the protection I provide you is gone, Emma, dear. She's free to kill you. As it is right now, she can't touch you. She couldn't even do this." Monique wrapped Emma in a hug.

The warmth and scent of spices wiped everything away. The cold of the Other was gone. The fear she'd experienced disappeared. Suddenly, Emma was crying, collapsing into the woman's embrace.

Mia joined them. After a moment, Leo added himself to the circle. Everyone wrapped their arms around each other. Emma couldn't tell where she ended and the others began. "One for all," she whispered.

"All for one." The combination of their voices gave her strength.

22

Well, that hadn't gone as I'd hoped. As soon as I saw my errand boy get smacked across the head with a vase, I knew my plan was sideways. Leo Ambrose's consciousness was difficult to get ahold of in the first place—the smart ones always were—and now I might have blown my only opportunity to get at Monique.

Frustration burned in my muscles as I ran through the trees, following paths I'd known since childhood. I detoured around the Place of Moonlight, where I'd left Monique a little "thank you" present.

Were it not for her, I would've accomplished a great deal more a long time ago.

Monique would never invite me to her location on her own. I'd had to orchestrate my invitation, and Emma played her role perfectly. And now I knew where Monique lived.

A tree branch snapped as I pushed through the brush, and I worried that Emma and her friends might be on my tail. If they were willing to take Leo down, possibly kill him, what would they try with me? Pausing at a stout oak, I panted and listened.

Nothing.

They could've been moving quietly, following the trail I'd blazed. Those two agents with Emma had carried themselves as if they knew the wilderness. Maybe the FBI trained its people better than the Salem PD, or maybe they'd picked up some skills on their most recent case.

I'd caught a few glimpses of Emma in the woods outside of Norell this past week. Nasty bit of work, that case. For a moment, I'd thought Emma would fall through some wilderness trap and, *poof*, that would be the end of her. Unfortunately, I was wrong.

I needed to get to my sanctuary, to *my* circle of power. It was much stronger than our childhood Place of Moonlight. My sanctuary allowed me to navigate easily between this earthly realm and the next. It was populated with Shades who energized me.

Controlling a few of the spirits and bending them to my will had been such a thrill the first time I accomplished the feat. I thought I had solved the riddle and found a way to make the Other fully and totally mine to control.

Rounding a tight curve in the path, I pushed between two trees and leaped over Damien Knight's body.

Poor Damien had slammed his head repeatedly into a tree trunk.

He'd proved useful beyond measure, committing my crimes and arranging the bodies in the Place of Moonlight.

Sadly, he couldn't be counted on to behave. His mind had a tendency to remember too much, even with my influence guiding him to my desired targets.

He'd taken out Mary Evert and Brittany Weir well enough, leaving the Evert woman's screaming brat and Weir's idiot husband exactly where he'd found them. And then, his usefulness had run its course.

Pausing once more to confirm I wasn't being followed, I scanned the forest around me for movement.

Not hearing or seeing anything threatening, I'd turned to go when a Shade rushed toward me. The wispy figure turned nearly solid in front of me, and I had to take one step back.

It was the ghost who'd been helping Emma a great deal, ever since he'd first appeared in February. Our eyes met, and I felt his desire to push against me, to force me away. With a simple gesture, I banished him, just as I had so many others over the years.

He spun away—revealing two bloodied bullet holes, one in his back and the other in his shoulder—and receded into the mists of the Other.

The effort wouldn't keep him at bay for long, though. He'd be back to help Emma soon enough. For now, my path was clear. More Shades swam around me, but none of them were actually concerned with my presence.

Things were going better than I'd hoped. Explosions, fires, and chaos spread in my wake—not from some magical display of power, but because I'd planned for this moment for years.

As a trusted police detective, I'd had access to homes, businesses, and even municipal buildings under the guise of my work. No one ever questioned my presence, my reasons for being there, or my seemingly innocuous inspections. Over time, I placed devices in key locations, quiet seeds of destruction waiting for my signal. I'd wondered if I would ever need them.

Now I knew I did.

A simple press of strategically timed buttons had been all it took this morning to turn Salem into a frenzy of chaos. Fires erupted in homes. Explosions gutted the police precinct, the community center, and even the city courthouse. Each detonation served its purpose, drawing attention away from me and ensuring the authorities were overwhelmed.

Magic might have given me power, but this…this was the result of meticulous human planning. My devices made it clear—I was more than a mind manipulator or a spirit wielder. I was always five steps ahead.

Even though my attempt at using Leo Ambrose had failed, I could still accomplish my task. I simply needed to reach my place of ultimate power.

Only Emma could trouble me there, and she'd have to find it first. Not even Monique knew of the place, the circle Gina and I had found all those years ago.

I crossed back over the barrier Monique had made. Now that I'd received my invitation to enter Monique's land from Emma, her invisible defenses had crumbled like those flakes of rusted paint.

Climbing into my cruiser and starting the engine, I whispered a final goodbye to the woman who'd never truly been my friend.

You were just another hanger-on, someone to drag Gina down with you instead of helping her rise to the prominence and majesty she deserved.

I turned back down the access road. Heading into the neighborhood bordering the preserve, I considered the best route to my destination.

My sanctuary, the most powerful circle in the area, lay southwest of the city. I chose the route that would take me around the heaviest rioting.

As I drove, I kept my lights running and chirped the siren as needed. No doubt, Emma and her friends would be radioing Chief Peterson soon, to report me and initiate a hunt.

Last Spell

Staying well away from the largest concentration of trouble would work for and against me. A stray police cruiser in the suburbs would be more noticeable with every available officer currently struggling to maintain order in the city center.

I followed a course through the neighborhoods south of Salem, hopeful that the chief's shelter-in-place order would work to my advantage.

Soon enough, I was on the roads I'd been prowling since Gina's first act of betrayal, when she became engaged to that idiot, Charles.

I entered a suburban street and had to brake for a little girl on a bicycle. She pedaled along, unaware how close she'd come to death, and I sat momentarily stunned by the sense of peace that emanated from the oblivious youth.

"You haven't a care in the world, have you, child?"

She finally noticed me, and her eyes went wide as she took in the flashing lights. She quickly moved out of the roadway, then turned and waved. I granted her a slight smile as I accelerated past her, wondering where in the hell her parents were and why they'd let her leave the house.

Not my problem.

The turn to my destination was ahead on the right, into the neighborhood abutting the largest forest preserve in the area.

I parked and got out, making my way down the street to the greenbelt.

Back then, the greenbelt had been a simple gravel path into the woodland behind the street. A golf course was added to the area a few years ago, the path widened into a two-lane thoroughfare.

My presence caught the attention of several people. Some were joggers, and others pushed strollers. I got a questioning look from a father carrying a child in a harness while holding a dog's lead. "Everything okay, Officer?"

"Detective. And, no. There's a shelter-in-place order out for the city. You," I motioned at all the people who were now slowing to listen, "should all be in your homes. Please get inside as quickly as possible."

Flurries of questions were hurled my way. I did my best to silence the voice inside that told me to just kill them all and be done with it. "Please! Everyone, Chief Peterson of Salem PD has the mayor's approval. You are to shelter in place. Go home, stay inside, and await further instruction."

Without waiting for their acknowledgment, I continued marching forward until I passed the turnoff leading to the golf course.

The paved path finally came to an end, and my shoes once again sank into the bare earth, carrying me to the place Gina and I had discovered all those years ago.

We'd sneaked out of Gina's house—not for any particular reason, Gina's parents would've let us go wherever we wanted—but we were young and looking to make a little adventure. It had been the kind of night where the air felt heavy and choruses of cicadas droned nonstop.

"Let's go exploring." Both of us were drawn to the woods. We'd walk around the periphery, but tonight, we had flashlights with fresh batteries and a spirit of spooky fun more appropriate for Halloween than mid-July. "I bet there's all sorts of cool stuff in there."

We only hesitated a second before we ducked under branches and scrambled over gnarled roots. We weren't as smart as Hansel and Gretel, though. We didn't mark our way, and soon, we were lost.

We wandered for what felt like hours, the canopy overhead growing thicker, the moonlight dimmer.

At first, it wasn't scary.

Then it got cold.

"Do you feel that?" My breath puffed out in front of me. I'd felt this before, this cold. Our other circle, the Place of Moonlight, which we shared with Monique, would drop in temperature just like this.

"Ghosts." Gina's face was pale in the flashlight beam.

Only a couple steps farther, and we entered the clearing.

It was round, like a fairy ring. Not quite as perfect a circle as our Place of Moonlight. Thick grass grew in tufts. A strange haze hovered in our beams.

Gina stepped forward first, toward the center of the circle. She was always braver than me. I followed. It was like plunging into an icy lake. The shock stole the breath from our lungs.

I kept my flashlight aimed at the trees, just in case any creature wanted to burst out at us. But everything was silent. No birds rustled in the branches. No rabbits scurried in the brush. I couldn't even hear Gina breathing. Or the cicadas humming.

"Do you see that?" Gina stepped into a bit of the thickest clump of haze in the clearing's center point...and disappeared.

"Gina?" I didn't think, I rushed to where she'd been.

If stepping into the clearing had been an icy shock, the bone-numbing air that swallowed me felt like I'd been dropped inside a vat of liquid nitrogen. My rib cage felt brittle against my lungs. I couldn't even move my jaw.

Shades were all around me. Some had normal faces, but others had died horribly. Necks twisted at unnatural angles. Chests bleeding with bullet wounds. They spoke, but I couldn't make out the words.

I fell backward, out of the haze, and landed on my butt in the clearing.

"Gina!" I was terrified. I didn't see her anywhere.

I whipped my flashlight around, searching.

I want Gina. Where is Gina?

The thoughts were fast and panicked. But I wasn't too confused to miss what happened next.

Show me Gina.

My flashlight beam bent at a ninety-degree angle back to the circle's center.

And there she was.

Her eyes were wide as they met mine.

"Whoa." Gina looked so...perfect. "Do you feel that? Do you see that? Did you see them?"

I could only nod. This place was special. Magical.

But Gina didn't seem to like it. Her face was pale, and her eyes looked like neon beams of blue light. Her irises were pinpricks in the flashlight. "We shouldn't be here."

My jaw dropped open. "Not be here? It's amazing."

"It's scary. Something is wrong *about it."*

I didn't want to go. I was no longer freezing. I felt weirdly safe here. I wanted to know why my flashlight beam acted so strange. Why Gina looked like an angel, even though she seemed to be scared. A million questions surged through my mind. Why were Gina's eyes so wild and blue?

Gina shook her head violently, her ponytail whipping her in the eye, and she fell from the haze onto the ground next to me. Her eyes were normal again. "No. I don't think we should be here." She stood. "We need to leave. Never speak of this place. We shouldn't even tell Monique. She'll be curious, and it's not safe."

"Okay, Gina. We can go. And this can be our secret."

She walked at a clipped pace back to the woods. I had to hustle to keep up, but before I entered the dense forest, I turned around to study the circle one more time.

I made my decision quickly. When I turned back to follow Gina home, I made sure to dig my feet in deep on the way back, marking the trail. I'd come again without Gina the very next day. I'd learn the route. The place would be mine.

That was the only secret we'd ever kept from Monique.

I stepped into my sanctuary, my place of power and focus—both of which I needed after trying and failing to get at Monique. I'd been so close. At least I'd broken through Monique's protective enchantments. It was only a matter of time now before I dealt with her…and Emma Last.

My girl, I will be seeing you very soon.

23

Emma sat silently in the passenger seat as Leo drove them back into Salem, watching him out of the corner of her eye. He'd recovered, mostly, from being knocked in the head. She was glad Mia hadn't put all her strength into the blow, otherwise they might've been forced to detour to a hospital.

But whether he had recovered from Celeste's manipulation, she couldn't tell.

They had the information they needed. Celeste was the Other-worldly villain they needed to stop.

After resolving the situation between her and Leo, Monique explained how Celeste's efforts at possession worked. She would use anything she could find that might connect a person to the Other, as a sort of conduit.

That could mean the ghost of a lost loved one, like Leo's grandfather, or the ghost of someone the person had killed with malice. Thankfully, as far as Emma knew, Leo had never taken a life except in the line of duty.

And the same went for Emma and Mia.

Monique said that could make you all vulnerable to Celeste, because she uses a connected ghost's lingering resentment to affect people and make them open to possession.

Emma suspected Leo had some kind of affinity for the Other. He'd come to her rescue during a bombing case, rushing into her B and B bedroom to stop her from jumping off the balcony. She hadn't been herself in that moment. She still didn't know why she'd been standing outside during a blizzard.

He'd said he heard a wolf howling.

Back at Monique's cabin, Emma had seen dozens of ghosts coming and going, and Monique had confirmed their presence every time she saw Emma's gaze dart off in random directions. *"They're happy to see you here, Emma. That's why more of them are coming around."*

None of them had felt like a threat to her.

Now, back on the roads through Salem, Leo wore a deep frown and slowed each time they passed more signs of violence. She hadn't wanted him to drive, but he was maneuvering well through the streets.

He'd been emitting endless sighs since they'd left Monique's, no doubt his sense of guilt over what he'd almost done.

He kept looking at his hands and rubbing them on his pants. But they were clean. They'd all washed their hands at Monique's. Emma made note to keep an eye on things like that.

"How do we find Celeste?" Mia leaned forward between the seats, focused on the road. "Any ideas?"

"I already checked property records." Emma held a hand over her mouth and nose as they passed a burning pile of garbage. "The home that went up in flames is the only one registered to her, and there's no record of any family, despite that bedroom in her house that looked like it was for a child."

Mia sighed. "But no kid pictures anywhere in the house.

She could've planned for a child, maybe, but never gotten pregnant. Or had a late-term miscarriage. The room was pink, suggesting a girl."

"Maybe. And if she lost a child at any age, I could see her wanting to keep the room in a preserved state." Emma pressed her palms on her thighs. "Sometimes, people deal with a major loss by pretending it didn't happen."

Leo tapped his hand on the steering wheel. "It sounds like the only family she ever cared about was Monique and your mom. Monique doesn't know where to find her, and your mom's gone. I don't know where that leaves us."

In the end, this all came back to Emma's mother. She couldn't risk reaching out to her mom in the Other, but maybe they could get something from the remains of Gina Last's life. "Leo, turn onto State Street up here on the left."

He narrowed his eyes but did as instructed. "Where are we going?"

Emma searched the side of the road as they drove, working at remembering landmarks she hadn't thought about in years. "My mom's the reason Celeste wants revenge, and the reason Monique cast a protective spell on me and drew Celeste's anger on herself. We can't question her, obviously, but it's probably time we went to my parents' old house."

Leo slowed for a railroad crossing, swiveling his head to check before accelerating. "So where's home?"

"About a mile away. Turn left up there at the barbershop and take Jefferson Avenue east. We'll cross a major intersection at Canal Street and go around the university's northern boundary."

From the back seat, Mia acknowledged the route. "I have the map up. Traffic monitoring seems to be working still. The roads are all red to the north, but things look clear around the campus."

Emma forced a smile that she didn't quite feel. "I want to say it'll be good to see home again, but…"

"You don't have to pretend for us." Leo reached a hand over to grip hers in a quick squeeze. "You have a reason for keeping the house in your family's name. Whatever that reason is, we won't judge you. You know that, right?"

She nodded and smiled again. This time, the act felt genuine. "Dad didn't want to sell it, and with the money I inherited when he passed, I never had reason to. I was so upset when my father died, I couldn't even bring myself to move anything out other than the personal items in his office. It wasn't safe to leave them unattended, but other than that, the house is untouched. I pay a service to go in and clean every month, so I can sell it eventually."

"But you haven't gotten around to it yet." Leo took the turn, following Emma's instruction to go straight after that. "You said your father's items weren't safe to leave at home? Why not?"

Emma shrugged. "My dad was a lawyer. It didn't seem right to leave his old case notes and files in an empty house for who knew how long."

"You think there's anything there that might help us find Celeste?"

"It's worth a try." Mia sat back in her seat, her voice a touch more confident now that they had a destination. "Until Jacinda gets here, I don't see what choice we have."

Nodding, Emma directed Leo to the next turn. They were just a few blocks from her old home.

Wheeling them around an abandoned skateboard and bicycle on the side of the street, Leo grunted. "I'm still not convinced Monique's innocent. She could still be the culprit, just doing a bang-up frame job."

He's really got it in for her. Why?

"It seems like the more reason we have to think it's

Celeste," Emma spoke carefully, meeting Mia's worried gaze before looking back at Leo, "the more you suspect Monique. Mind telling me why?"

"What, because I'm supposed to have all the answers?" Leo's face went blank for a moment, but then he shook his head and said nothing further on the subject.

Emma directed him to her old address just up the block.

As the house loomed into view, colonial and majestic, Emma's gaze remained on Leo.

He seemed to be losing track of his own thoughts, unable to explain his conclusions or keep his temper in check. And normally, he didn't even have a temper when it came to interacting with his colleagues. She decided to ask Mia to take over driving duty after this.

A memory of her father flashed to the forefront of her mind. She eyed the old maroon shutters and stately front porch, where he used to stand and greet her when she came home from school in the summer.

Emma bit back a sob, forcing herself away from the image that always came rushing back to her.

This place was the last earthly home for both her parents. She wanted to believe at least one of those deaths had been natural.

Leo parked squarely in the driveway, and they all stepped out.

Welcome home, Emma girl.

24

Emma had gotten a keypad installed on the old home so the cleaning service could come and go at will. The code was her mother's birthday. She typed it in and held the door open for her colleagues.

The warm oak floors gleamed in the light coming through the windows, and Emma's heart caught in her throat mid-beat. The old house looked just like she remembered it. Formal dining room off to the right, French doors to her father's office on their left, and a short hallway that led them into the open-space living room and kitchen where she'd spent so much of her childhood.

In between boarding school stays, you mean. You're romanticizing this place, Emma girl, just like always.

Maybe she was...but the spirits of her parents were haunting these walls. At least, she assumed that to be the case, and she reminded herself to be respectful.

Her mother's ghost would've been here for much longer, of course—Emma's whole life, really.

Emma recalled countless memories of her father listlessly drifting through the halls. Was he also wandering from room to room in death, as if he might find his wife hiding out somewhere, lost in a good book?

All her earliest memories of him were the same. His face drained of all life and color, almost as ghostly as the beings Emma saw in the Other.

She opened the doors to her father's office, showing off the space emptied of all personality. Most of the contents had been sent to her storage unit down in D.C. "We can look in here if all else fails, but I don't think we'll find anything."

"Where's our best bet?" Mia glanced around, down the hall and on into the heart of the home. "Did your mom have an office?"

"A study." Emma's voice cracked. "But Dad cleaned it out and turned it into a gym. There's nothing in there but old equipment. Our best bet's the attic or their bedroom."

The thought of riffling through her parents' belongings after all this time seemed almost treasonous to their privacy, but Emma supposed she'd already begun her riffling back when she'd found that picture. Not to mention searching out her mom's old friends. But she'd wanted to uncover secrets, hadn't she?

Well, this was her chance to find some more.

She led Mia and Leo down the hall and into the open-space portion of the first floor. The area was neat and well-kept, but obviously not lived in, and she hurried them forward to the wooden stairs that climbed up to the floor where their bedrooms and her mom's old study had been.

"There's no basement, but there is an attic. Let's start there." Upstairs, Emma hesitated at her parents' room, but then moved on toward the door to the attic. "There's a lot of space, and I have no idea how much stuff is up there. I'm just glad the space is still standing after all the chaos Salem's been through this week."

Mia glanced along the hall of closed doors behind them.

"Should we split up? You could go through your mom and dad's room, while Leo and I go up to the attic. If you want some privacy there?"

Heat thickened in Emma's throat. "No, let's stick together. We might as well."

Unlike the rest of the house, the attic was musty and dark, but the light bulb switched on obediently when Emma pulled the cord. Her gut twisted at the sheer amount of stuff surrounding them. Boxes on boxes of stuff were stacked in every corner and against every wall. Some of it she recognized immediately—the old plastic containers full of Christmas ornaments and lights, for instance—but some of the boxes were tattered at the edges and thick with dust.

Leo gazed around wordlessly as Mia stepped in closer to Emma. "Do we just start searching? Anything you want us to avoid? Like, uh, personal stuff?"

Emma forced herself to shake her head. "My personal stuff was moved out long ago, maybe with the exception of some old toys, but I bet those were given away. We should go through all of it, in case we can find anything related to Mom and her friends."

"Monique and Celeste." Leo spoke their names quietly and turned on his phone's flashlight as he headed toward a far corner.

Emma watched him for only a second before heading for the opposite corner, and Mia moved toward the window and the boxes surrounding it.

Part of her expected some ghost to appear and direct her, but unlike in the rest of Salem—and as much as she *felt* haunted while being in this old home—no ghosts did. The air and atmosphere remained slightly warm and muggy in the attic space, some degrees warmer than outside, and Emma soon had to pull off her overshirt and tie it around her waist to avoid breaking into a real sweat.

Hunting through boxes, she mostly found books and old clothes. She'd donated most of her dad's clothes to a local veterans' service, but one box held sweaters that must've belonged to her mother. She made a mental note to come back and look through it more carefully at a later time. She and her mom were about the same size, and it would be nice to have some of her old sweaters to wear...if just for the sake of nostalgia.

Aside from clothes, she sorted through books, a box of old tax records, and multiple boxes of records related to the house, ranging from home insurance and mortgage documents to roof repair and appliance warranties.

She'd been slightly wrong about her personal belongings being gone, as discovered when Mia found a whole box of art she must've made in grade school and when Leo found a treasure trove of ancient yearbooks. But they were soon down to only a few boxes, aside from the Christmas bins that Emma saw no need to revisit.

Mia had gone through multiple boxes of crochet patterns and yarn left from her mother's old sewing days, but they'd found nothing else that could be tied all the way back to the young Gina Taylor or Monique Varley or Celeste Foss. Those boxes would've been very old compared to these others, brought from her mother's parents' home.

Finally, Emma drew herself up and glanced back toward the doorway, knowing exactly what made sense. Mia pulled one of the unexplored boxes closer and nodded at her. "You go ahead. Leo and I will finish up here."

Leo yanked another box toward him that, if she guessed right, held nothing more than ancient magazines.

Halfway down the stairs, Emma stopped mid-step at the sight of Oren's ghost standing outside her parents' bedroom. His face appeared wizened, his eyes hooded, but he nodded at her, and a little ache built in her chest.

Last Spell 167

He disappeared before she reached the door.

Her parents' old bedroom beckoned, and she couldn't put it off any longer. Feeling herself in something near a daze, she went to their door. For a half second, she had the insane urge to knock—and very nearly lifted her hand to do so—but even if the spirits of her parents were inside, her father stationed in bed reading and her mother sewing by the window, it was far too late for her to worry about disturbing them.

Emma put her hand to the knob and turned it, saying a little prayer as she pushed the door open.

The room was spotless—the large area rug as bright and blue as ever, the wooden floors showing the thinnest layer of dust. The cleaners must've been through recently.

A lamp by the tableside was recently dusted, and the curtains were parted just enough to allow sunlight into the large, cheerful space. Emma's gaze caught on her parents' wedding portrait, placed above the bed, and her eyes stung before she turned away to face the closets.

Her dad had only ever used one, and she moved to that one first. As expected, the space was nearly empty. At the foot of the closet, some pictures leaned against the wall, but when she bent to examine them, she discovered they were all certificates of recognition from his old bowling league. Otherwise, the space was empty.

When she turned to the next closet, she was nearly paralyzed by heartbreak.

This had been her mom's space, and she remembered the day her father had attempted to clean it out.

Her hand hovered at the doorknob of the closet, wondering whether he'd ever finished. She never dared ask, no matter how many times she thought about it.

She turned the knob and pulled. Most of the clothes were gone. A single garment bag hung far to one side, but Emma didn't need to open it, and she wouldn't unless she got desperate. Calligraphy stitched on its side proclaimed it to be from a local bridal shop, and seeing her mother's old wedding dress wouldn't exactly help her get her emotions under control.

The shelf at the top of the closet held two very old-looking shoeboxes. She pulled both down and sorted through them in quick order. One contained pictures of her mother's family, most of whom Emma didn't recognize.

In the other box, she found an assortment of miscellaneous items...odd board game pieces and scraps of paper with her mother's handwritten notes on them. She found lists of everything from grocery items to party invitations to household chores, all penned in Gina Last's fast script.

Taking two of the grocery lists, Emma carefully folded them and stuck them in her pocket. She'd be able to use the lists for handwriting analysis.

The bottom of the box was inexplicably littered with a wide assortment of buttons.

Refilling the boxes and putting them back in the closet where they'd lived for decades, Emma sat down cross-legged in front of the items spread across the foot of her mother's old closet. A variety of small boxes and old puzzles had been tugged into half-sagging piles, though one whole corner of the space was devoted to the old crocheting supplies her mom once used.

Emma made quick work of sorting through two more boxes of photos—mostly of herself and her dad—before she hit on another older box. Her heart rate sped up as soon as she spotted the return address on the first letter in the stack. The name *Celeste Foss* stared up at her as if embossed in gold rather than black pen.

Tugging the letters from the box, Emma made sure they were sorted by their postal date before she began reading.

The first few letters had a friendly tone to them, and the dates suggested they must've come during high school. Emma could almost find it quaint that Celeste felt a handwritten letter was preferable to just talking in the hallways at school.

But the text of the letters made it clear why Celeste had chosen that mode of communication. She was trying to ensure secrecy from Monique. The letters were all addressed to Emma's mom as if she and Celeste shared some private code of solidarity, separate from Monique.

The earliest letters described their "sisterhood" and relegated mention of Monique to "our common friend."

Finally, Celeste's messages took on a more urgent tone, especially in letters dated around the time when Emma's mom would've been dating her dad. In one, Celeste described her "sanctuary," which she referred to as "Lorn Meadow."

She all but pleaded with Emma's mom to join her there, away not only from Monique but from *"everyone who continues to obtrude on our sisterhood."*

Emma's blood ran colder as she read Celeste's words. The space seemed far more potent than the Place of Moonlight, with a deeper and more powerful connection to the Other.

In another letter, Celeste remarked on a particular bonding rite she wished to conduct with Emma's mom at the new circle.

"With the power of this sanctuary, we will always be eternally whole. I can't tell you how good it feels to write that, Gina, and to know you feel the same way."

The phrase "eternally whole" leaped out to Emma. The same phrase appeared on the back of the photograph she'd found showing her mother, Monique, and Celeste together.

But that photo was taken before Celeste had distanced herself from the other women.

Hoping the letters might add to Monique's explanation for that schism, Emma continued reading. The more she read, the more she cringed with Celeste's tone changing from enthusiastic to near rabid fascination with the power she was able to experience in her personal sanctuary.

In another letter, sent when Emma's mother was away for the summer, Celeste urged Gina to return early, so the two of them could celebrate alone.

"I need you to come back to Lorn Meadow with me. I've discovered something amazing there."

Emma began to see a trend. *Togetherness* and *sisterhood* were the most common themes, but Celeste had excluded Monique every chance she could, especially once she discovered the place she called Lorn Meadow.

After reading a few more letters, Emma understood why. Celeste began referring to Emma's mother as her "closest blood sister."

With trembling hands, Emma found the letter dated the day after her parents married. Celeste's anger bled off the page, and each word was like a pin poking her skin.

Gina! How dare you write, 'Did you really expect me to never fall in love and marry?' Seriously? After the years we've spent together? Did you not think about what that would mean for my life? We took a blood oath. Of course, I expected that you wouldn't get married! You're a woman with her own power, just like me. Even Monique can claim the title. Have you told your precious husband that?

Ours was a magical pact that we entered into freely and as a rite of passage. I believed the vows we spoke meant something.

Your Sister in blood,
Celeste.

The last letter was dated around the time when Emma must've been conceived and included only a single line.

Gina Last, you will pay for your betrayal. I have been to Lorn Meadow and enshrined my vengeance upon you.

The letter was unsigned, without even a return address, but Celeste's writing was unmistakable.

With fingers that trembled more than she liked, Emma tucked the letters back into their box, working to catch her breath.

One thing was clear. Lorn Meadow was the center of it all. If Celeste was planning something big, that was where they'd find her.

Now we just need to figure out where the place is.

25

Leo tried to be open-minded about the letters Emma found. He did. But realistically, everything sounded like bullshit, and he didn't understand why Mia and Emma didn't see the truth just as easily as he did.

He paced the kitchen, while Mia sat on one of the barstools, and only half listened as Emma ran through the history she'd uncovered in her mother's closet. An angry cloud that had begun to fill his mind when they were in the attic grew heavier and heavier, but he didn't care. If anything, the skepticism overtaking him, along with the anger, only helped him see the truth.

"Leo, don't you want to see the letters?" Mia caught his gaze from across the island, an insipid smile on her face. "This is—"

"Bullshit."

Her face went white.

He didn't care. "This lead is bullshit, Emma. Hell, the whole situation is bullshit! All we've been doing is following you around your hometown, going on a stupid ghost hunt, while the city has devolved into a war zone! I don't know how you two are living with yourselves, examining family heirlooms when we should be helping people!"

Emma's expression tightened, reminding him of Jacinda when she got hot under the collar for no reason.

She faced him head-on like she was his boss, which she most certainly wasn't. "You want to calm the fuck down? For someone who said he'd support me, you sure don't sound supportive. Or like yourself at all. Given what we witnessed at Monique's earlier, I'm not sure I like the idea of you offering an opinion."

"Fine, Celeste got into my head somehow. But she's not there now." Leo leaned forward over the island, ignoring how his raised voice made Emma take a solid step backward. "I have control of my faculties, Emma, and news flash about opinions. They're like assholes, remember?"

She and Mia rolled their eyes at him. "The best you can come up with is schoolboy jokes? Now I know you're not in 'control of your faculties.'"

"Really?" He smacked his palm on the counter. "Well, when did you and Mia start letting your imaginations run away with your brains? You want to answer me that?"

The horror Leo felt at the venom spewing from his mouth was like nothing he'd ever experienced. He couldn't control it. As much as he wanted to believe Celeste wasn't in his head any longer, he now knew otherwise.

He couldn't do anything but clench his hands and grit his teeth against the emotions tearing his chest apart.

Leo twisted around, unable to face their dumbfounded silence, and stalked toward the sink, where he splashed water over his face. When he stood straight, dripping and gasping, they still hadn't spoken, but the heat of their judgment at his behavior sizzled his skin.

"We need to get back to Monique's. She didn't tell us everything, I'm sure of it." He faced them again and ignored the wrenching pain in his gut that came alongside the distrust and anxiety on their faces. Distrust and anxiety brought on by his own words and actions. And yet, he still couldn't curtail his anger.

Emma's mouth opened first. "I—"

"Are you two listening? We actually know where Monique is, unlike Celeste, who may or may not be in this stupid 'sanctuary.' What'd you call it? Lone Mountain?"

"Lorn Meadow."

"Whatever. Hell, those letters are how old?"

Emma opened her mouth to speak again, but nothing came out. Her hand came protectively down onto the letters she'd stacked on the counter.

"I'm right, aren't I?" Leo laughed, deep and long. The sound grated on his own ears, but he couldn't stop the ridicule coming through his words. "It's a wild-goose chase, girls."

Girls? Did you seriously just call Emma and Mia "girls?"

Mia took a tiny step toward him. "Leo, I—"

"Celeste might be the one behind all the trouble, but weren't your mom and Monique just as 'powerful?'" He added a flippant air quote, his words dripping with more and more condescension. "Why is Monique suddenly making you do everything, Emma? Why can't she just tell us what's really going on? So, yeah, that's where I stand. This whole thing is utter bullshit."

His words ground to a stop, and he stared at the two women in front of him. Emma appeared shell-shocked. Stunned. Unable to speak. Mia's eyes were so wide, they reminded him of how Yaya used to tell him and his brothers to pop their eyes back into their heads when she found them staring at something.

My mind's not right. It's not. Why can't I tell them that?

Because the words still wouldn't come. No matter how

much he wanted to address the shock on their faces and apologize for most of what he'd just said—if not every single damn word—he couldn't make his lips move unless it was to release some kind of vitriol or verbal abuse.

Repeat it to yourself. Repeat it, and maybe that'll help.

I think she might be doing something to my mind. I think she might be doing something to my mind. This isn't me. She's doing something, I think. This isn't me. I think she must be doing something to my mind.

He repeated it like a mantra, and his blood ran hotter and hotter with frustration that the words wouldn't come, but nothing made any difference. Mia stared at him for a long moment, her mouth opening and closing, until she finally excused herself and went to the bathroom.

Emma's jaw tightened, a vein throbbing at the base of her throat. She stalked over to the window, carefully tucking the letters into a pocket.

Irrational rage spiraled through Leo at their silent distress. His head began aching, though he still tried, forcing himself to continue the mantra he'd built.

But it made no difference. The words simply wouldn't come.

Then I won't talk. I won't say anything else hurtful. I just won't.

Leo turned back to the sink, washed his face again, and stood working to slow his heart rate. Hoping that, sooner than later, he'd have control of his own mind and words again.

Even if that didn't happen immediately, though, he wouldn't allow himself to be sidelined from Emma's fight. He might not be able to tell Mia and Emma that Celeste was still in control of his mind, but he'd fight to maintain control of his body and actions in silence.

He *would* still help Emma. There'd be no more arguing against her, belittling her or Mia, or opposing them.

Determined to be there for his friends, to support them just as he'd promised, he closed his eyes to center himself.

A sudden vision flashed before him. A symbol painted in red blood. Clearly occult, though he couldn't read it. His blood chilled, and his muscles froze.

Am I seeing through Celeste's eyes? Like Monique talked about seeing through spirits to talk to Emma?

Casting a look around, he noticed features similar to those in the Place of Moonlight near Monique's cabin. Only this circle he was seeing didn't have three dead women lying in the middle.

Only Celeste.

She held her arms out to her sides and stood with her face to the sky. Her lips moved, but he couldn't catch what she was saying.

What he could see were the droves of ghostly beings swarming toward her, moving en masse like a body of water trapped in a vortex.

He was among them, moving without a will of his own. No matter how he tried to fight the sensation, his feet surged him forward. Leo felt himself sway and looked down at his body. He was standing in place, but he saw the faint image of a red coat, like those worn by the British during the American Revolution.

Resisting the pressure that drew him ever closer to Celeste, Leo tried to be an impartial observer. He looked to his left and right. All around him were the ghosts—the Shades—of people who'd been in and around Salem over the centuries.

Soldiers from the revolution, American and British both. Some Hessian troops, still wearing their metal cap plates even as their bodies leaked blood and viscera from the wounds that'd ended the war for them.

Leo saw a group of women, all wearing the garb of early colonists, their necks broken by the hangman's rope.

A young boy who had been struck by a car staggered past him, one leg bent awkwardly behind the boy showing tire tracks on his pants leg.

Leo was closer to Celeste now, unable to avoid the pull of whatever she was doing. An icy cold gripped his heart, and his chest seized as he struggled to draw breath.

Celeste's head snapped in his direction, her frozen white eyes like two warning beacons. In that instant, he wound up like a pitcher on the mound and shot his energy at her, pushing himself in the opposite direction.

He was propelled away from her, as if he were inside a playback being run in reverse. Celeste grew tiny in his view as he was flung back down a trail leading away from the circle surrounded by so much blue. Trees snapped by on either side of his vision, then his view was nearly inverted as he began rising up a hillside.

Leo slid between two massive stones at the top of the rise, but they quickly vanished as he was flung even farther away, down the opposite slope and through more trees, sailing across the greens and sand traps of a golf course and finally emerging into a suburban neighborhood.

The last thing he saw was streaming lines of ghosts pouring onto the trail he'd just been evicted from. He could think of no better way to describe the sensation he'd just experienced.

His vision dimmed until the ghostly world he'd been in disintegrated around him, leaving him shaken and alone.

Breath died in his throat as he pictured the hordes Celeste had been calling to herself. Hands grabbed at him from somewhere, and he screamed, trying to get free.

Leo's eyes snapped open. He was back in Emma's house, standing in front of the kitchen sink. Mia and Emma had their hands on his arms, holding him upright.

Emma gave him a slight shake. "Leo! Leo, we're here. You're back with us."

A wet cloth wiped his forehead. Mia released her grip on his arm and applied both hands to the cloth, holding it over his brow.

"She's…" Try as he might, Leo could say no more. He needed to warn them that Celeste was at Lorn Meadow, recharging her power and gathering a horde of dead people…

They were so far in over their heads, so far beyond anything they understood.

But he couldn't make his mouth form the words to tell them.

26

Emma pushed Leo into a chair, fighting to get her breathing under control.

"I'm gonna take a minute with Mia, okay?" She turned away from him even as she noticed the words land in his expression with just the tiniest flinch.

"We're a team, Emma! We're…" Leo's voice died on his lips when she didn't turn around, and though part of her ached to apologize for shutting him out—even after all he'd said—this wasn't the time.

Celeste had managed to find a way into his mind, and they needed to be prepared for the worst. If he suddenly turned rogue, they'd have to use any means necessary to ensure their own safety as well as his.

When Mia came out of the hall bathroom, Emma nodded toward the front of the house. She opened the French doors to her father's office, ushered Mia inside, and closed the doors behind them.

Mia was red-faced, having given herself a wash similar to Leo's, but her eyes were narrowed and worried. "What the hell was that? Do you have any idea what's gotten into him?"

Facing the doors, ensuring their privacy, Emma spoke quietly. "Listen, if he goes off the rails again, we need to take him down and cuff him."

Mia perched on the windowsill. "I want to know we can trust him. I feel like he's trying to stay in control, but something's getting in the way."

Emma knew exactly what was happening. "Some*one*. It's Celeste, using the Other to bring him under her influence, just like Monique did for me back in Buckskin. Only Celeste's not able to maintain the connection because Leo has no interest in being controlled by any other person. No interest in being part of the Other."

"Like you."

"Yeah. Like me."

Even though she'd at first thought of him as the inferior replacement of her old partner, Keaton, Emma had trusted Leo practically since she'd met him. And yes, she'd seen him lose his temper on their first case together. He'd flown off the handle at the slightest indication that the old circus ringmaster was abusing a child who was a member of his troupe.

Leo had been wrong in that case, admitted it, and come back to his senses. But his recent attack on Monique, and his behavior just now, was so far out of character that she was prepared to treat him like a suspect until she could guarantee he wouldn't spin out again. "Should we cuff him and put him in the back of the car?"

"What, like a perpetrator? I know he nearly killed Monique, but that wasn't his own doing. You and I both saw his eyes go white back there. Just like Brittany Weir and Officer Konig."

"And look what happened to them. We need to take his gun." Emma gazed past Mia out the window. The others who'd turned violent had done so quickly, attacking without warning, just like Leo had done with Monique.

And Celeste forced Konig to take his own life.

"Let's get his gun from him. I think we have to."

"Agreed." Mia crossed the room and put a hand on the doorknob. "That's what we do, right? We keep an eye on one another."

Back in the hallway, Emma closed the French doors and followed Mia to the kitchen. They found Leo perched against the counter with a sheepish expression on his face.

"I'm sorry…" He looked like he fought for words but then gave in to some other impulse. "For everything. In general. I'm stressed out and worried. That doesn't excuse anything, but it feels like the cause. Don't give up on me."

The itch in Emma's mind that had told her he was still susceptible to Celeste's influence went quiet. "You still with us?"

"Always." He stood straight, wiping his already clean hands on his jeans as if to start a new task, symbolically if nothing else. "I'm committed to helping you and helping Salem. I think you're right. We should look for Lorn Meadow. I'm ready when you are."

Concern ate at Emma still, tingling at the back of her mind, but she nodded. "Apology accepted, with conditions."

"Conditions?" He looked between back and forth them before settling his gaze on Emma. "Which ones?"

The question hung in the air for only a moment. "I'd like to have custody of your weapon, just in case. Will you willingly surrender it?"

He stared at them, visibly shaking, as if fighting against some urge or thought he wished he wasn't having. Leo's hands remained at his sides. He tilted his head, as if he were considering something someone had said, then it snapped upright.

Fight her, Leo. Fight, fight, fight.

His left hand rose slightly, catching at the hem of his jacket and lifting it aside. "Take it. Quickly."

Emma moved without hesitation, sliding her hand inside his jacket and pulling the gun free. She backed up a step, holding the weapon behind her.

She and Mia slowly backed away from Leo as his left hand spasmed once before slamming against the countertop behind him. He let out a tortured cry. Emma saw Mia reach her hand inside her jacket to the cuffs she kept on her belt.

Leo put a hand to his chest, breathing hard but finally settling down. He darted a look around the kitchen and shook himself. "I'm fine. I'm me again. We can go, and I know how to get us there."

"You what?"

"I saw the path, when Celeste was inside my head earlier. There's a golf course and a very nice path. It's paved. Then I saw two big rocks on a hill. There's a clearing in the trees on the other side of those. It's one of those circles, not far from the rocks. And there was a lot of blue."

Emma touched the letters in her pocket.

She wasn't certain they could trust Leo to guide them into Lorn Meadow with this description of a golf course, paved trails, big rocks, and "a lot of blue," but it was all they had to go on.

If Leo was right, with any luck, they'd soon end this once and for all.

27

There wasn't much time.

I'd been tracking Emma and her team for a while now, and I knew they'd be like dogs with bones as they hunted me down. Hell, that damn Special Agent Leo Ambrose somehow got into the Other, even without me consciously trying to bring him over.

It was probably Emma's old boyfriend again, making trouble. He's been doing that since he first appeared, and you've never been able to affect him except to send him away.

He'd shown up with the ones I'd called to me, but I banished him as I'd done before, and Leo along with him.

I sat in the center of my sanctuary, with an old hat upturned in my lap. The haze swirled around me, thick and cloying, a veil between worlds. A doorway to the Other. I was untouchable at Lorn Meadow. Invincible.

A stack of nine-millimeter bullet boxes sat next to me. These were the last I'd managed to grab from the precinct. Now that the station had burned to the ground, no one would notice them missing. Over five hundred rounds in all.

I'd been robbing the armory for the last few years to create my stockpile, slowly and methodically, one box at a time.

I opened one and dumped the contents into my palm. Reaching in with both hands, I cupped the bullets together, clutched them like a mother spider might hold her brood, and called out to the Other as I thrust my hands forward through the icy barrier.

From the first moment I'd entered this sanctuary alone and staked my claim, I realized it was more powerful than the Place of Moonlight. The Other had a special property I could use to my advantage beyond communing with ghosts here. If I stepped through the veil and focused on a living person or place, I would see them in real time. And once I could see them, I learned how to control them. Which took time, but it'd been worth it.

More recently, I'd discovered that certain objects could gain certain "finding" properties, if I focused on them while in the Other.

Denizens of the Other swarmed to me, as they'd always done when I entered Lorn Meadow and called out to them. They were at my whim. But now, instead of finding purchase in me, I called the Shades *into* the bullets I cradled in my hands.

I shivered against the chill flooding my fingers and wrists, crawling up my arms, until the last bullet was infused with the Other's nature.

I no longer had a choice after what Gina had done. She'd dared to weaken our bond by getting married and having a child, forever committing her attention and her love elsewhere, outside our bond.

After Gina abandoned me, I would often come here to watch her, but Monique's infuriating protective spell made her location fuzzy. Emma's, too, though I'd tried multiple times. Once I'd gotten *so close* at a bed-and-breakfast location. But I'd ended up closer to her friend Leo.

More recently, though, when her colleague almost died, drifting into the Other, I could see Emma through the haze.

"Denae, you heard me! I said come back. Right now!"

Always so close, and yet so far away. I'd howled with frustration every time.

I lifted another ammunition box and emptied the bullets, clutching the rounds in my cupped hands. My fingers grazed the icy boundary of the Other. It parted like a gossamer spiderweb. I plunged my hands through once more, gritting my teeth against the searing cold.

In the Other, everything was different. Sharper and fuzzier at the same time. I felt the energy rattle through me, a brittle pulse.

I focused my thoughts on the bullets, picturing them in my mind's eye. I imagined them in flight, sleek and deadly, unerring and unstoppable. I saw them burying themselves in flesh, puncturing skin and shattering bone.

As I withdrew my hands, pulling the bullets back to the real world, they were wrapped in tendrils of haze. The collection of brass and copper in my palms throbbed with a silvery light, alive with malevolent purpose. As I'd done before, I returned them to their case on the ground beside me.

I sensed a disturbance at the edge of the clearing. There were Shades everywhere, wandering like the lost sheep they were. If they knew all they had to do was ask—or demand— to visit a person or place, they would've left the netherworld long ago. I imagined that was why so many of these spirits were victims of violence.

As a police officer, I'd seen the terror and confusion on victims' faces. It was no surprise they might get lost after something so traumatic.

Standing between the Otherings, pulsing with Other energy, was that irritating boyfriend of Emma's. He was only there a moment, not even long enough for me to flick him away before he vanished on his own.

"Good riddance." I lifted the next box and dumped it. Leo was more difficult to control than I'd imagined, especially if he was being helped by beings I had no power over. I might still be able to confuse or befuddle him, but I suspected his usefulness was growing thin.

Gradually, the stack of Other-infused ammunition grew.

Years ago, as a patrol officer, I'd conducted an experiment. A series of robberies had drawn excess media attention, and my department was certain that the same group of individuals was responsible. By then, I was tired of those crooks making us look like fools.

So I came up here, put an ammo box through the veil, then loaded my service weapon with the bullets.

My partner and I intercepted the robbers at a liquor store. They opened fire. I'd taken shelter behind a cement guardrail across the street. I couldn't get a good bead on any of them. But I'd lifted my gun in the air and fired three times. The whole time thinking, *Hit Robber One, Robber Two, and Robber Three.*

I'd seen where they'd been shooting from and visualized their positions as I fired. Every one of my shots found its mark.

Experiment successful.

Listening to the chatter on the police radio, I smiled at the chaos I created. Pulling a secondary phone from my pocket, I opened an app and selected yet another site for an explosion.

ATF was on their way. *Good luck.*

I glanced over at my new stack as I replaced the most

recently imbued loads in their box. This would be more than enough for Monique, Emma, and her little FBI helpers.

And where were those three musketeers right now?

I stepped into the Other's haze to find out.

28

Howard Blackwood flicked the curtain most of the way closed in his front window, retreating into the darkness of his home. The fires and sirens and shouting kept interrupting his thoughts. He looked at the chess game he'd been playing against himself, set on the card table beside his fireplace.

What's the point of playing anymore? It's not like I can count on Miller or Consuela to come by and challenge me to a match again.

The damn shelter-in-place order meant he couldn't go outside or down to a neighbor's house for a chat. Not that he'd want to step out his own door with all that madness, but he was a lonely older man, and those relationships were everything to him.

Howard's only other friend, Phoebe Wilson, had died at the hands of a psychotic idiot just a couple days ago. The idea of being stuck in Salem with nothing but crazies for company hung like a weight around Howard's neck.

Who would be his bridge partner now?

Who would he call when he needed help with a

crossword? No one else would put up with him when he wanted to spend the entire afternoon at the all-you-can-eat Chinese buffet in town, course by course and plate by plate, only to follow that up with a single glass of plum wine poured over green tea ice cream.

Nobody was as good at crosswords as Phoebe had been.

What a friend. Not to mention that they'd understood each other and bonded over their deceased spouses and dogs. Sharing memories even as they drowned in them.

But now he was truly drowning. Howard picked up a crossword book and stared at a puzzle for a moment. None of the clues seemed anywhere close to answerable, so he put the book aside.

Out the window, three government-looking types stood by a beat-up Malibu.

Life was a lot easier when he was younger, like those three dummies standing across the street right now. He didn't think they were cops—they seemed a smidge too educated and young and pretty—but they had the look of law enforcement, at least. Federal officers of some sort, he guessed. The man's hair was too long for them to be military.

Howard wondered what they were up to. If they were Feds, shouldn't they be getting the damn city under control so he could safely go outside again?

He'd seen the fires on the news. He'd been lonely and depressed for so long, it was almost a relief to see the world crumbling around him.

As Howard watched the trio of police or agents or whatever they were, a haze of anger began settling inside his mind.

That woman with the black hair turned in a circle and pointed at a few things like she was bird-watching. Then she turned back to the other two and just…smiled.

Smiled, for pity's sake! What gave her the right to smile when the world was falling apart?

Depression had been a mainstay in Howard's life for decades. But now rage slipped over him, more profound than any sadness he'd ever experienced.

It's soothing to lose control. I feel freer. I never thought about it like that. Not once...until now.

Moving faster than he had in years, Howard ignored the ache in his knees and hurried toward the entrance to his garage. There, he plucked up a rag set aside for dusting—as if a clean house mattered in this damn world.

He went to the liquor cabinet. Though he'd been meaning to pour it all out for years, he just couldn't bring himself to take that step. Even though he no longer touched the sauce, just having the bottles around gave him a sense of ease.

Of power.

He could take a drink now, but that would be wasteful. The booze had a more important purpose.

Howard uncorked the bottle of rye whiskey he used to love so much and stuffed the rag into the neck, bit by bit. He had to get a wooden spoon from his utensil drawer to really get it in there until it reached the amber liquid inside.

Giving the bottle a good shake, he got the rag nice and soaked, until he smelled the rich sweetness of the rye on the end that hung out of the bottle.

Before he stepped out his front door, he lit the rag with a match and let it burn as he walked down his drive toward the stupid trio of lazy Feds.

As he marched toward them, his grief melted and the pain in his knees all but disappeared. This would be a good end.

The woman with the flyaway light-brown hair noticed him first. She held up a badge and shouted. "Stop. FBI! Throw the bottle aside!"

"FBI!" Howard cackled, more life in his voice than he'd felt in years. "I was right!"

The agent drew her gun. Howard grinned, feeling the embrace of death warm his bones.

He cocked his arm back, but before he could throw the bottle, it exploded in his hands. Flames erupted and raced up his arm, searing his clothing to his flesh. It was okay, though. This was supposed to happen. He felt like he should finish his job—run at the people who had intruded on his street, in his life.

He took a staggering step, but the searing pain spread across his shirt and ran down his sides as flames licked at his face and scorched his flesh.

Howard's smile melted into a confused frown as he looked down at the fire.

He was useless and stupid, then that feeling winked out like a candle being snuffed.

Now the only thing Howard knew was pain.

But, mercifully, not for very long.

29

Emma holstered her gun, her gaze fixed on the burning body.

Mia yanked a garden hose from beside the man's garage—assuming he lived there—and stood on the sidewalk, spraying the flames, but the man was beyond saving.

When his fate was no longer in question, she dropped the hose and came to stand beside them. "That attack was directed at us. He didn't exactly look like a man accustomed to murdering anyone, let alone people with guns saying they're FBI agents."

"No, he didn't. And his eyes were white." Emma swept her hair back from her face, cringing at the smell of smoked flesh now carrying on the breeze. "We're being attacked directly and can expect more."

"I'd say this means we're on the right track." Mia looked over at Leo, who only grunted in response. "We need to figure out exactly how to get to Celeste's sanctuary."

Emma thought of the description Leo had given them of where Lorn Meadow was located. She'd brought them back to Celeste's neighborhood, because where else would the point of origin be if not her home? There were one or two golf courses sort of nearby, but no trails or wilderness extended from around the neighborhood, and not a hill could be seen in any direction.

A few neighbors were coming out of their homes now, drawn by the commotion, and Emma nodded toward them. "I need to look at a map to figure out exactly where we need to go. Can you two keep a lookout while I do that?"

Leo snorted. "You don't want me to chauffeur you around some more?"

Great. Now we have a Worry about Leo *column. Check, check, and check.*

He'd been quiet on the drive over from Emma's childhood home but had started grumbling once they'd parked. She ignored his comment. "I'm going to sit in the Malibu and look up other locations on my iPad. Narrow it down before we start driving all over."

Leo waved her back to the car. "Yeah, go. We should conserve gas anyway. With all the chaos, we might not be able to find a functioning pump if we start getting low."

With nothing but accusations on her tongue, which would be of no help now, Emma let his attitude slide. She tucked herself into the front seat and pulled up a map of Salem on her tablet. She began searching for golf courses located near anything that might have some elevation to speak of. Most of Salem, even the wilderness preserves near Monique's cabin, was pretty flat.

The terrain west of the city rose to higher levels, with more wildlands in that direction.

Emma zoomed in and began hunting for golf courses with trailheads and small mountain ranges nearby.

Bless Salem's city government for wanting hikers to know where to go anyway.

There were multiple courses butted up against wooded

areas but only one with a greenbelt pathway at the back of a neighborhood that linked up with a trail network. The trails ran around a municipal golf course and through a woodland preserve. It was southwest of Salem proper, a neighborhood where her mother had grown up. That was the point of origin—her grandparents' home.

This has to be it.

They knew where to go. Now they just had to get there.

But the most direct route to the greenbelt access point would take them right through the worst areas of violence in Salem.

Or they could detour south of the city and take a highway into the next town, approaching the neighborhood and greenbelt path from the opposite side of the woodland preserve.

She was about to set down her tablet and inform the others when Mia let out a high-pitched shout that was followed by a gunshot. Emma dropped the tablet on the floorboard and jerked out of her seat.

Outside, a man lay bleeding on the street near Mia, shot at center mass. The rest of the neighbors had backed off but remained on their lawns or driveways, watching.

If Emma gauged their expressions correctly, they were angry or frightened, but none of them seemed broken up about the body on the street, though she couldn't parse out any white eyes.

By the time she reached her friends, Mia was in Leo's face. "What were you doing? Why weren't you there?"

"What…" Emma glanced down at the knife by the man's outstretched hand.

Mia whirled on her. "Leo was right there! Right there! And this man nearly stabbed me in the back, and he didn't do anything! I didn't have a choice. I had to shoot."

Leo stood blank-faced, his mouth opening and closing as if searching for words.

He's getting worse, Emma girl. You have to finish this before Celeste takes him over completely.

Mia followed Emma's gaze and seemed to wilt before her. "Do you know where we need to go?"

Emma nodded and took a step toward the car while keeping one eye on the gaggle of angry neighbors whose mutterings were getting louder. When Leo didn't immediately move to follow, she wrapped a hand around his bicep, and he moved after her obediently.

Somehow, that didn't make her feel better.

"Mia, you feel like driving?" Emma handed her the keys, then all but tugged Leo toward the passenger side. While Mia adjusted the driver's seat—Leo looking a bit shamefaced now—Emma retrieved her things from the front passenger seat and gestured to Leo to get in. "More legroom. You're taller."

He didn't argue, and Emma didn't miss the nod she received from Mia. Someone had to keep an eye on Leo at this point, and that would be easier if he were in the front with one of them in the back.

Emma kept watching the neighbors, who remained where they'd been, observing and shouting at them but not engaging in any outward violence. "There's a trail system southwest of Salem. Go back around the campus and take a left."

Reaching forward, she typed the location of the trailhead into the GPS before belting herself in. They'd just have to leave the car on the side of the road and hope for the best once they found the way in.

Mia got them moving and out of the neighborhood. Within minutes, they were cruising through nearly deserted city streets. The shelter order had some lasting effect here, at least.

With Emma navigating and Mia steering them around the occasional wrecked car, they exited Salem and made their way into the suburbs. The roads outside the city were more peaceful, almost as if Celeste's home really had been the epicenter of violence and destruction.

Leo's phone buzzed. He picked it up and looked at it, then dropped it into the cup holder beside his seat. Emma tapped his shoulder. "You want to answer that?"

He only grunted in reply, mumbling something about a headache.

Mia cursed beside him, hitting the gas a touch harder.

Emma leaned forward to look at Leo's phone, glimpsing Jacinda's name. Flashing the screen at Mia, she answered the call without bothering to put it on speaker.

"Hey, Jacinda—"

"Where the hell are you?" Jacinda's voice blasted through the car. "And why are you answering Leo's phone?"

"Uh, he's not feeling well. We're still in Salem, but—"

"Well, we just landed in Boston, and the first thing we were greeted with was a video of some crazed old man trying to light you on fire before blowing himself up! I have someone working on getting the damn clip off YouTube as we speak."

Emma cringed, barely able to imagine what their SSA must've been thinking upon watching that scene unfold. Of course someone had been recording them. Unbelievable.

She took a breath, trying to keep her voice even as she responded. "We're following a lead outside of town. I think we have a bead on the person behind all this."

Jacinda's voice was muffled for a moment, and Emma finally put the phone on speaker for Leo and Mia to hear. She might need Mia's help navigating this conversation after all. "How can one person be causing this, Emma? What do you think is going on here? As far as we can tell from our end, we're looking at an outbreak of chaos. Random acts of violence."

Emma swallowed down the urge to tell Jacinda everything. It wouldn't help, but how else was she supposed to explain her thought process?

Mia waved for Emma to angle the phone in her direction. Trusting the urgency of the gesture, Emma thrust the device between the front seats.

"It's Mia, Jacinda. Emma's right about the lead. We think it's an infectious agent that's causing people to act out violently even where they have no cause. We're trying to get to the person behind the dispersal before things get worse."

Emma's eyes went wide. That was brilliant. She mouthed *thank you* at Mia and focused back on the phone while Jacinda communicated what Mia had said to Vance. "We have a lead on the location, Jacinda. We just need some time—"

"Uh-uh, Emma. We'll go at this together." Jacinda breathed out loudly, and Emma heard Vance arguing with someone in the background, demanding more reinforcements. "We're heading in from Boston momentarily. Give me the address for the nearest police station, and we'll meet there."

Emma braced herself, then steeled her voice. "Please, don't ask us to do that, Jacinda. Look, even if the nearest police station hadn't gone up in flames, which it did a couple of hours ago, we'd be wasting time. It'll take you over an hour to get here from Boston, and we can be where we're going in fifteen minutes or less. We can't delay, or it might cost lives. Please, let us follow this lead. If it doesn't get us anywhere, we'll meet up with you as soon as you're here."

For a moment, Emma thought for sure Jacinda was about

to order them to stand down. But then she conceded. "I'd prefer you wait for us. But you're right. We're looking at an hour plus just to reach Salem."

Jacinda muttered something on her end, maybe calming down Vance from the sound of things. "Do you have PPE? Whatever you need for protection from anything this person might throw at you if you find them?"

A breath released from Emma's chest, hard and fast. "We're prepared."

Not technically a lie.

"All right." Jacinda sighed, and the sound of vehicles zooming by came through the phone. "We're heading to pick up our rental now, and we'll be there as soon as we can. Send me the address?"

Emma glanced up at Mia, nodding. "We're heading to the general area now. Soon as we have an exact location, you'll have it."

"Good enough. Be safe, okay? That's the first priority. And if that means you wait for us, you damn well better wait for us."

Jacinda's voice was so gruff, Emma didn't know whether to laugh or be touched. In the end, her throat clogged with emotion even as she replied as simply as she could. "Thanks, Jacinda. You all be safe too."

When the call ended, Emma dropped the phone back into the cup holder beside Leo. He'd barely acknowledged the call, still holding one hand against his temple.

And that said everything about the situation they were in.

They'd just cleared one hurdle, but it had been a small one.

More than just fear and nerves gripped her now.

Anger rippled through her mind, growing with each little fib they'd had to tell.

Celeste Foss wasn't just messing with Emma. She was messing with one of Emma's closest friends and forcing her to lie to her other friends and trusted colleagues. If the woman wasn't already running…Emma was about to make her wish she had.

30

Leo's head ached with pressure.

The anger building in him could no longer be separated from even his most casual thoughts. A shift in his periphery reminded him that Emma was in the back seat now, strategically placed to keep an eye on him.

And Mia was driving, though she almost always preferred to ride passenger. But Emma couldn't drive just in case her cold spells came back, and neither of the girls—*women*—trusted him.

Mia dodged their beat-up car around a group of people waving signs alongside the sidewalk, though they couldn't be mistaken for normal protesters. Their signs were bullet-ridden and singed, and a lot of the protesters were waving knives or garden tools in the air. One lunged at the Malibu with a rake as Mia passed, but she sped forward, and the protester could do nothing but scream at their taillights.

Leo fought the urge to giggle at the man's anger. Anger was funny. And a rather pleasant emotion to witness. Downright comical.

He turned his head toward Mia so he could side-eye Emma.

She was mostly focused on her tablet, eyes down. They'd spent so much time building up trust over the past months. And she'd told him more than once that she was his friend. But now, watching her, he didn't particularly know why he'd bothered.

What was she? An overly focused FBI agent who put herself on a high horse and happened to be able to see ghosts? She'd nearly allowed herself to get killed, only to be saved by him on more than one occasion, and now he was following her around like a lapdog? Why?

Maybe because of what you saw in that...place in the woods? Wherever you went to earlier, when you saw Celeste again.

The pressure in his head flared, and he flinched back into his seat. A voice in his head begged him to relax.

"You need to let go."

He immediately pictured Celeste, but the pain grew so intense, he had no choice but to concentrate on that instead.

That voice returned. *"Why fight it? What's the worst that can happen?"*

It was Celeste, and her voice was a soothing balm against the burning pain. He shifted in his seat, muscles tensing as he fought against the ache.

"Just let go." She was more forceful but still sounded motherly.

He relaxed, and that was when another notion entered his mind.

He wanted Emma Last dead. He wanted to see her fail, spectacularly, and then he wanted to see her die.

His gut recoiled, but his mind pushed forward—showing Emma collapsed on the ground, leaking blood. Showing her on fire and then tied to a tree and with a knife jutting from her chest, eyes wide and bloody. Her death was beautiful and necessary.

No. Emma is...my friend. I don't want this.

Pressure exploded behind his eyes. He rubbed them with his palms.

Leo grabbed for the only thing he could think of that might help him fight off Celeste's attack. A memory of his first case with Emma, when they took down a murderer targeting members of a traveling circus.

She'd seen the ghosts of the victims during the case. Emma used what one ghost told her to distract the killer.

Emma had saved a young woman's life that day. Saving lives was the reason Leo had joined the FBI in the first place. That was his whole reason for doing anything.

She's just as good as you, just as capable. Better, even. And she's...your friend!

Mia asked him if he was okay. He forced a grunt of acknowledgment that hopefully sounded like reassurance. His mind roared with pain when he did, though, like someone had thrust red-hot pokers in through his ears.

Each time he shoved away the picture of Emma being murdered—being tortured and then slain—a sharp pain swirled through his brain.

That's what'll happen if I keep fighting this. My mind will be torn in two. It'll burn up like an overheated hard drive.

The thought held truth, and it weighed heavy on him as a new image of Emma pressed forward. In this one, she was smiling. Grinning, in fact. At her feet, Denae lay sprawled and bleeding out, begging for his help, as Emma stood there, laughing.

Denae's eyes welled with tears, and Leo's own grew hot in response. Watching his love plead for help sent tendrils of misery racing through his chest.

Her last breaths bubbled from her lips in a bloody froth as Emma did nothing.

"Emma isn't worth helping. She's the one who let Denae get shot. Don't you remember?"

"She tried to hide her glee, but you saw through it. Denae almost died because of her, Leo."

"How could you possibly want to save her?"

"Emma Last deserves to die, and you know it."

Leo felt helpless, just like when he'd held his hands over Denae's wound to staunch the flow of blood. It just wouldn't stop. The directives in his mind battered him relentlessly—though he tried to put pressure on them, too, using good memories of Emma.

With that comparison, his willpower left him, and he was free. Clearheaded and ready for what had to be done.

Emma wasn't someone who deserved his help. She wasn't some sweet, innocent capable of making the world a better place. She wasn't the kind of person his yaya had raised him and his brothers to be. She was an ulcer on the side of the Bureau, weighing all of them down. An enemy.

My enemy. I see that now.

And while he couldn't eliminate her this very second, he could begin planning and working toward her ultimate demise.

The very thoughts entering his mind made Leo gasp for air, but he couldn't backpedal from them now. It was all he could do to keep from pulling Mia's weapon from her holster and turning it on Emma.

I could turn it on myself. Before I kill her.

The thought sent a white-hot lance of pain down his spine, and he clutched his head and groaned. Emma murmured something, but he couldn't understand her.

And then it was too late. His mind walked into the fog, wholly and completely.

Leo smiled to himself.

My eyes must be turning white. I can't let her see that.

He aimed his gaze out the window, then made a show of shielding his eyes from the sun so the girls would understand why he took his sunglasses from his pocket and put them on.

With his eyes shielded, he allowed himself a glance back at Mia and smiled.

She hesitated, but then smiled back, and he thought he saw some freedom in her eyes. The same freedom he felt, now that he'd learned the truth about their colleague. Perhaps she was beginning to see what needed to be done too.

Because, yes, he absolutely knew what needed to be done. No more wavering. And when the opportunity came, he'd be ready. Leo eyed the butt of Mia's gun peeking out from inside her jacket.

Not yet, but soon.

The protector, Monique Varley, had to die first.

Then it would be Emma Last's turn.

31

Emma's every nerve had gone on high alert since Leo had put his sunglasses on, but as Mia drove to the end of the suburban street and parked, she turned her focus to what was coming.

As it was, Leo relaxed in his seat with such an ease that Emma wondered if he was thinking of anything at all, let alone the supernatural mission set before them if they wanted to save Salem. Assuming he was still in his right mind, they didn't have long before Celeste stole him away from them, just like she'd stolen so many other citizens of the city.

What Emma didn't understand was how. Celeste lived by Damien Knight and Brittany Weir. She worked with Michael Konig. It made sense to her that Celeste could be in close proximity to them and get inside their minds—or even somehow magically do it just because she knew who they were.

But she hadn't even met Leo when he started exhibiting signs of no longer being in charge of his own thoughts, feelings, or actions. He'd started acting strange on their way to Monique's cabin the first time. Before he'd met either woman.

Mia unbuckled her seat belt and glanced from Leo to her. "This is it?"

"This is Salem proper. I'm pretty sure, yeah." Emma climbed out. She thought it would look more familiar.

Mia followed along beside her. They spread out in opposite directions, away from the vehicle, eyeing their surroundings, particularly the woods at the end of this cul-de-sac.

A sudden cry from Mia rent the air. "He took the keys!"

Emma spun around to see her friend scrambling to get up from the ground, her pants dirty and her hands scraped up, just as Leo sprinted back to the vehicle.

She flung herself after him with Mia just a step behind, but Leo was faster. He slammed the car door, woke up the engine, and jarred the car into reverse just as they reached it. Then he swerved back down the roadway.

Heart pounding, Emma pulled her gun and aimed for the tires, but Leo had already sped out of range.

Her mind spun, struggling to figure out next steps. "We need to go on without him, but I say we alert Jacinda that we're separated."

Mia shook her head. "Veto on Jacinda. You want to try and explain what just happened?"

Emma kicked at the ground. Pain shocked up her leg. "No. I want it not to have happened at all." Before she could consider other options, a Dodge Challenger came speeding into view from the other direction.

As one, Mia and Emma pulled their badges and stepped into the middle of the road, hands up to signal that the driver needed to stop. For a moment, Emma feared he wouldn't, but he skidded to a halt some twenty feet away.

Emma approached, ready to draw her weapon in case the man was another of Celeste's minions.

The door opened, and he got out. His eyes were ghostly white as he aimed an accusing finger at them. "Rotten Feds! Stealing my tax money, that's what you do. And for what? Good riddance!" He reached into the car and came out with a shotgun.

Emma drew and took her shot, hitting him in the arm.

Flying backward, he dropped the gun and let out a wail fitting for a horror movie.

But then, that was what Salem had become—a horror movie, rife with unreasonable violence and bloodshed, forcing her to shoot innocent people. Exactly what she wanted to avoid.

Gripping his shoulder, the man groaned. Before Emma could decide whether to cuff him or offer him real aid, he looked up at them, anger dripping from his now-normal eyes with clear brown pupils. The gunfire must've jolted him back to reality. He stood and ran off before they could offer him help.

Her hand shaking, she holstered her gun. "Well, that was interesting."

"At least we have transportation." Mia yanked open the passenger door of the Challenger and swung herself inside just as Emma dropped into the driver's seat and fastened up. "He didn't even turn it off."

Emma hit the gas before Mia had buckled her seat belt. She pressed down on the pedal so hard, the engine roared. "You thinking what I'm thinking?"

"He's going to Monique's. I don't want to think about what he'll do when he gets there either."

Emma squealed the tires, taking a corner, for a moment feeling more alive than she had in days with the power of the Challenger under her control.

Back on the main road, she watched for Leo's taillights. "Keep an eye out for him? I'm going to take us on the fastest route to Monique's."

Mia acknowledged her with a "yep."

They were heading directly toward the heart of the chaos in Salem, which was still the quickest way through town to Monique's. But just as Emma signaled to change lanes, Oren appeared in the rearview mirror. He was in her back seat, aiming a finger at the road ahead.

"He's going to protect her. Circle back at the next off-ramp." Oren smiled at Emma as he continued to point before disappearing.

They sped past the first exit into town.

"Where are you going? Monique's place is past town!" Mia's shocked voice broke in on Emma's thoughts.

"Oren was just here. He said something about Leo 'going to protect her' and said to 'circle back.' I think he meant Leo was going to be Celeste's protector, the way Monique is ours. And Celeste is likely at her circle. The plan stays the same. Find Lorn Meadow."

Mia glanced her way, frowning. "And you still feel okay? You're not getting chilled or…summoned, like on the last case?"

"I'm fine." Emma swallowed hard, then floored the engine. "I mean, as fine as I can be, all things considered. Celeste isn't getting to me, as far as I can tell. What about you?"

"I'm good."

Emma had no choice but to take Mia's word that she wasn't being affected. Without knowing the length and depth of Celeste's power, the only way either of them could be safe was to keep checking in. With Monique alive, Emma was protected, but without knowing how this happened to Leo, was Mia safe?

"Just tell me if you start feeling Leo-ish, okay? And I'll do the same."

Mia grinned sadly as Emma turned off and headed into the neighborhood just south of where they'd previously been. She didn't have time to study the homes, but it did have a sense of familiarity she hadn't felt moments earlier in the other spot.

"Look!" Mia aimed a finger down a neighborhood street they'd just passed.

Emma slammed on the brakes and backed them up, irritating another driver who had to veer around them to prevent a collision.

Maybe fifty feet down the street to their right, Leo had parked their Malibu at a greenbelt entrance. "Parked" was a generous description, because the car's front end was wedged between two bollards set up to block vehicular access.

Emma wheeled them over and pulled to a stop along the sidewalk just before the greenbelt entrance. They got out and approached the now very much ruined Malibu, weapons at the ready.

"Leo? Are you in there? It's Emma and Mia. We're here to help."

While Mia approached from the passenger side, Emma moved up alongside the driver's door. She saw the vehicle was empty. Thankfully, no bloodstains or spatter marked the interior, meaning he'd merely driven the car in between the bollards and become stuck.

"He didn't crash, at least. Any sign on that side?"

"Nothing here. Just those sunglasses he put on."

Emma checked the car's interior again and saw them. He must've torn them off and discarded them. They sat wedged between the windshield and dashboard on the passenger side.

A quiet, familiar voice broke into Emma's thoughts, and she almost cried out with joy. Monique had reached out to her through the Other, and unlike the last time, when Emma had been in the middle of a forest, now she could hear the woman as if she were standing beside her.

Hearing Monique's voice coming from nowhere was a shock she quickly shook off.

"Where are you?"

"Nearby. Is it safe to come out?"

"Yes." Emma spun around, looking for the woman.

Mia rounded the Equinox's front end with a question on her face. "Who are you talking to?"

"Me." Monique emerged from the greenbelt path, having used a stand of bushes for cover. "When I reached out through the Other and saw Leo had been taken, I knew I had to come quickly."

"How'd you get here?" Emma holstered her weapon and greeted her mom's friend with a brief hug.

"I followed some friends. I believe you know one of them. Oren?"

That made sense, but it still didn't explain how Monique had physically made the trip. "I mean, did you drive or...fly?"

Monique let out a tinkling laugh. "If only things were that easy. I drove my truck." She pointed, and Emma saw the old green truck parked down the block. "I hoped I could get here before Leo and intervene, maybe help him resist Celeste's influence."

"We're pretty sure we know where he's going. We just don't know how to get there."

"Celeste's private sanctuary, yes? I'd caught some of his mutterings when I reached out through the Other. He kept mentioning a place called Lorn Meadow."

Mia had moved over to the greenbelt trail. "Are we going after him? He could be under Celeste's control, but he's unarmed. He has no way to fight back, even if he does break free somehow."

"I would advise against going after him. When I encountered Oren, he said Celeste has been manipulating Leo all along. Oren tried his best to intervene, but she's too strong for him and keeps forcing him away. Wherever she is, she has a terribly strong connection to the Other and is bending it to her will. You won't be able to fight her there."

Shit. This was a "take two" from earlier. "Celeste is probably counting on us thinking like that, wouldn't you say?" Emma scrubbed her hand over her face. "She pulls Leo here, knowing Oren has been helping us. Of course he'd tell us where she is, and now we have no choice but to continue. She has Leo hostage."

"Yes, and she plans to use him against you." Monique rubbed her arms, though it wasn't cold. "Or me, more likely, since my protection remains in place over you and Mia by default, long as she sticks by your side."

"So why did you come here at all?" Mia's question landed with the weight of a prosecutor's final statement. "Why not just stay home, where you're safe and can keep protecting us?"

Monique turned to her, eyes rounded with conviction and determination. "Because Leo is also Emma's friend, and my protection alone wasn't enough to prevent Celeste from getting into his mind. The three of us together may be enough to stop her, though. We have to hope so anyway."

Monique was risking her own life to save Leo's too.

"We'll find him, and we'll protect you. Let's get moving."

"Thank you, Emma dear." The woman reached a hand over and gripped Emma's upper arm for support as they stepped over the Malibu's now-detached bumper. "I do hope you're right."

Emma motioned for Mia to fall in on Monique's other

side. Her chest tightened as they stepped onto the greenbelt path. As they ventured into the woods to find Lorn Meadow, she had no idea what would happen next.

32

At first, the three of them stepped carefully along the pathway that cut through the woods, looking for signs of Leo's passage. Emma had to laugh at the irony of tracking a colleague on the heels of pursuing a cannibal through another wilderness area.

Remembering what Ranger Harley Feeney had shown them, Emma examined the earthen path for disturbed leaf litter and shoe marks, and she encouraged Mia to keep her eyes at a higher level, looking for broken branches or torn leaves.

"Just like old times." Mia's joke fell flat until Emma spotted a tangle of tall, dry grass recently smashed down to the ground.

Monique stood to the side as they moved closer to inspect the damaged foliage.

"Someone came through here, leaving the main path. One guess as to who it was."

"I'm going with a six-two, shaggy-haired FBI agent with Greek ancestry."

Without warning, the air tightened, and Emma's arms

shook with a deep, clutching chill. She bent forward, hands on her knees, gasping with the pressure of the Other-thickened atmosphere and the cold.

The chill cut deeper along her spine, and Emma twisted her head to glance backward. Monique must've felt it, as well, because she'd stiffened where she stood and her eyes clouded over, going milky white with the Other's presence.

"Monique? What's going on?"

The woman shook and swayed a moment, then snapped her eyes shut. When they opened again, they were back to her natural icy blue.

Shouting and screams from deeper in the woods got all of them on alert. One familiar voice rose above the rest.

"That sounded like Leo." Emma looked to Mia, who nodded.

"It did, and he sounded like he's in trouble."

Moving in the direction of the yelling, Emma checked on Monique before getting too far off the trail. "Are you coming?"

"I can't keep up, dear. You and Mia go ahead and know that I'll be behind you." She waved them on. "My protection will be in place, no matter where you are. Just wait for me before you attempt to confront Celeste."

Emma gave her a short nod before turning back and sprinting through the tall grass. She went up a slight rise with Mia behind her, then dodged between two stout trees, listening for more shouts from Leo.

His voice echoed around her, then seemed to turn off like a siren cutting out. Emma pushed forward through the dense trees, occasionally checking back to confirm Monique was following the path they'd taken.

The older woman with her flowing shawl picked her way between the trees, moving at a snail's pace by comparison.

Slowing only enough to ensure they didn't lose Monique

entirely, Emma drew her weapon and scanned the forest around them. As she jogged on, she nearly tripped over a fallen tree but caught herself on a branch. Mia held out a hand for her to regain her balance.

Behind them, Monique paused to catch her breath. She looked so small from that distance. Mia patted Emma on the shoulder. "Up ahead. Leo said he saw two rocks in his vision, right?"

Emma turned and peered through the dense stand of trees and bushes. Two enormous boulders stood like soldiers protecting the top of the hill, with just a narrow gap between them. The ground dropped away on the other side of the mammoth stones.

Mia stalked forward, her gun out, muzzle down, keeping pace with Emma as they moved through the dense undergrowth. "Leo's here, right? I haven't heard him again."

"Neither have I. His voice kept cutting out back there, and now he's gone silent." Emma spared a final glance back at Monique but couldn't see her through all the foliage.

"Do we go in opposite directions and loop around the boulders and down the decline behind them?"

"Carefully." She stepped around the boulder closest to her. Mia mirrored her.

They met on the opposite side and stood at the top of the decline.

Mia considered the way down. "Do we keep going? Have Monique follow closer?"

Emma opened her mouth to answer but froze when the sharp snap of a twig echoed behind them. She turned, peering through the gap between the two boulders.

Leo appeared from the trees with his arm encircling Monique's neck from behind. A gun pointed at her temple. Emma's hand went instinctively to her waistband, where his weapon was safely tucked.

Celeste must've given him one. Shit, shit, shit.

"Leo, stop!" Mia's voice was demanding, but Emma knew her well enough to hear the crack of fear in her words. "Put the gun down. You don't mean to hurt her. Monique's innocent, and you always protect the innocent." How the hell he'd gotten to Monique in the first place without them seeing or hearing him was another question for another time.

Emma stepped forward, interrupting the standoff. Monique's panicked eyes were wide, terror radiating from them.

"Leo." Emma left her gun holstered, taking one small step after another. No way could she shoot Leo even if she had a bead on him. "Look at me. *See me*, Leo."

He snarled at her, and then stuttered his gun against Monique's head.

The woman whimpered, clutching at his arm, and he yanked her backward another step, keeping the boulders between them and Emma.

"Leo!" Emma raised her voice, stopping where she was and waiting until he looked at her. She threw her best dagger. "What would Denae think of you right now?"

Leo's shoulders bunched. He narrowed his eyes on her, as if confused. And then he repeated the name. "Denae? What would...Denae think?"

"You love Denae. The two of you care so much about each other." Emma's voice faltered, and she took another step to mask the emotion aching in her every pore. "Denae wouldn't want you to do this. What would Denae want you to do?"

Leo froze where he stood, Monique pressed against his chest. His breath seemed hard and labored. But he moved his gun away from her temple, letting it dangle by his side. He stumbled forward, still holding Monique by the crook of his arm.

When he was on open ground, Emma lunged between the

boulders to meet him. She clapped her hands around his gun and twisted it from his grip.

He brought his other arm up, releasing Monique. She stumbled away from the two of them as Emma grappled with her friend.

His gun thudded on the ground. Emma kicked it away, toward Mia. Planting her back foot, she propelled Leo toward the boulders.

"Leo, it's me! Emma!" She clutched his wrist, squeezing tighter even as he grunted in pain and punched her in the kidney. She danced away with the blow, gasping for breath. "Think of Denae, Leo! Denae!"

He fell against one of the massive stones, and Emma bent over to catch her breath.

Leo clutched his head, screaming. "Leave me alone! I can't…I can't…I can't tell what's real. Get away! Emma, get away!"

Emma's breath caught in her throat, but before she could find a response, Mia called out from behind her. She and Monique stood several feet apart. The older woman had her hands up in a defensive posture. Mia was holding both her gun and Leo's. She had them aimed at the ground as she shook her head violently.

"I'm feeling strange, Emma. Strange and wrong." Mia's voice was weak with confusion, just as Leo's had been in the woods when he'd first felt Celeste's reach.

Mia held out the guns by their barrels. "Take them. Before I do something I can't control or stop."

Emma crossed to her, took the guns, and stuffed them into her waistband. Standing between Mia and Leo, Emma swung her gaze back and forth between them, watching her friends fight against Celeste's influence. Monique dropped to the ground, mumbling quietly to herself as she sat in a meditative pose.

Emma gripped Mia's shoulder. "Breathe deep. Think about where you are, Mia. Think about Ned. About Sloan. Think about Vance. It's gonna be okay."

Leo sobbed out Denae's name, and Emma twisted to look at him. He stumbled away from the boulders and collapsed against a slender tree trunk, clutching at it for support. From the agony in his expression, there was no doubt he was fighting for control of himself.

And maybe winning.

Still...

Not allowing herself time for hesitation, Emma hurried toward Leo, even as Mia kept struggling against Celeste's hold. She ducked behind the tree and caught his wrists, slapped a cuff on one, and pulled his other arm around the tree, latching the other cuff before he could resist. But in his fractured state, he almost seemed to appreciate what she'd done as he sagged against the tree.

"Sorry, friend. We'll have you out as soon as we can." She gripped his shoulder briefly, but he only grunted in response.

When Emma stood, Mia met her eyes for an instant before falling to her knees, clutching her head. "Emma...it feels like there's an angry cloud pressing in on me."

"Inside my head." Leo's words might as well have finished Mia's thought. "Pressure."

Mia moaned. "I can't make it stop!"

Emma hesitated. She could cuff Mia to the tree, too, but what if she needed her in the coming fight? Mia seemed to be resisting Celeste's call better than Leo.

She searched out Monique's gaze. The other woman remained where she'd sat, still quietly muttering.

From the woods, the sounds of footsteps cracked branches and broke leaves, growing louder and louder. *Shit.* Since they were closer to the epicenter, did that mean her powers were increased and she could control more than two people at a time?

God, I hope not.

As the first white-eyed person emerged, Emma left Mia uncuffed and moved closer to Monique.

She had to protect the woman if they were going to survive.

33

Emma glanced over at Mia, who crouched on the ground, clutching her forehead. Turning to Monique, Emma reached for the woman's shoulder. "Is there anything you can do to help them? There are at least a dozen people coming at us through those woods."

Monique brought one hand up to clutch the crystal pendant hanging at her neck. "I'm trying to help your friends avoid turning fully to Celeste's side. Leo fighting her off like he did is a good sign that it's possible, Emma, dear. I'm doing my best."

With that, Monique went back to her muttering, which Emma now realized was some sort of chant. She faced the forest as Celeste's minions moved steadily forward.

Her first thought was to check all four of her guns for ammunition, but she had no justification for shooting civilians.

These people don't know what they are doing. Their minds are literally under someone else's control.

Remembering her own experience with mind control, when Monique had pulled her into the Other, Emma did her best to concentrate on seeing the people around her as the victims they were.

The first soldier reached the edge of the hilltop clearing. He carried a broken tree branch like a club and swung it back and forth as he stalked toward Monique.

Emma stepped into his path and pushed him backward, not wanting to injure him if she could avoid it. He took a lazy swing at her, but the branch came nowhere close to hitting her.

Monique's voice raised in pitch. Her chanting became forceful and insistent.

The man with the branch stumbled over his feet and fell down, rolling from side to side on the ground, as if struggling to resist whatever was happening in his head.

Just like Leo. He's being attacked in his mind, but there's enough of him in there still that he can fight back.

"Sir! Sir, I need your help. You have to fight against the voice or whatever is trying to make you hurt people."

He relaxed for a moment, as if hearing her, and his grip on the tree branch weakened enough that she could yank it from his hands and toss it to the side.

Leaving him there, Emma focused on the sounds of the other footsteps crunching through the brush and undergrowth among the trees.

The next two puppets to come into the clearing were young—teenagers, maybe. A pair of elderly women came behind them, all of them following a path toward Monique.

Emma dodged in front of them, placing herself between the would-be assailants and the one woman whose presence seemed to guarantee Emma remained immune to Celeste's manipulation.

With a grunt, Mia lurched to her feet and came to stand beside Emma.

At the same time, the man who'd wielded the tree branch

stood up again and collected his weapon. He lunged, swinging at them.

Emma pushed him aside again as Mia shoved the teens back a few steps, which only made room for the older ladies to come forward. They moved sluggishly, their features warped with looks of utter confusion.

Even with their eyes a ghostly white, Emma could tell the women did not want to be anywhere near the hilltop, much less on a collision course with Monique or a young, strong, trained FBI agent.

Behind them, Leo wailed, but Emma shoved the sound away and focused on grappling with the old women as gently as she could. "Ladies, please. We need your help. You need to fight the voices you're hearing, not us."

Mia repeated the plea, calling for the teens to fight back and resist. The man with the tree branch swung at her, and Mia dropped to her knees, dodging the blow. She recovered and brought him down again by kicking his legs out from under him.

As Emma focused on the pair of young people, who apparently decided not to rebel, a deafening howl split the air.

On the heels of it, an agonizing cry of pain rent the air.

Emma whirled around to find a man on top of Monique, his arm raised, a large rock clutched in his fist, ready for a killing blow.

More footsteps sounded from the woods. "I'll take them!" Mia cried out. "You help Monique!"

Emma seized the man attacking Monique. She caught his arm just as it began a downward drop and used her momentum to tackle him to the ground.

She landed on top of him, fighting for control of the rock. The nails of his free hand bit into her arm as he fought her, but she ignored the pain until she gained control of the makeshift weapon.

A civilian screamed behind her, and Mia screamed back, but Emma couldn't look. The man was scrambling for the rock she held, clawing at her with both hands. She used her free hand to strike him on the chin, hoping for a knockout punch that would let her get back to helping Mia.

When her fist connected, the man's eyes flickered, and the ghostly whiteness faded, replaced with bright-brown pupils.

Emma released a giant breath of relief and pitched the rock away. She stood up and offered a hand to help the man stand. He rubbed his jaw and looked behind Emma. His eyes flared wide. "Watch out!"

She spun to see the man with the tree branch slamming it over Monique's head as she sat there, chanting.

The branch cracked against her skull, knocking her chin into her chest. Monique's body shuddered, and she slumped to the side, blood matting her gray-brown hair against her scalp.

Mia barreled into the man, knocking him onto his stomach so she could cuff his hands behind his back.

With a chorus of startled cries and gasps, the rest of Celeste's army stumbled back, the white film fading from their eyes as their irises returned.

Emma's heart dropped. *Celeste did it. She accomplished what she's always wanted to, so she's letting these people go. She doesn't need them anymore because—*

Monique!

Emma collapsed beside the fallen woman and carefully placed her onto her back.

Her eyes flickered open and shut. "Not all hope…is lost. Emma, it's okay."

Emma clutched her hand, trembling with adrenaline and emotion. "Monique, you'll be—"

"No. I won't." The woman coughed. "I won't be. I won't… and the protective spell will…be broken. But all hope is not lost…"

Emma gripped her hand, waiting for her to explain, but Monique's eye's fluttered closed, and her fingers slackened in Emma's grasp.

She was gone.

34

The civilians milled about one another, demanding answers. Some of them took out phones and tried to make calls, but they must've been far enough into the wilderness that signals were spotty.

Emma listened Mia attempting to explain the situation without going into supernatural specifics.

Despite having known the woman for only a short time, Emma couldn't help feeling like she'd lost someone close to her. On some level, Monique had represented a connection to her mother—a real, tangible one—and she'd been a protective force in Emma's life. One way or another, she no longer doubted that. Not after everything she'd seen in the most recent attack on herself and her friends.

Several feet away, though Mia was doing her best, the crowd was getting antsy. Emma sensed they weren't buying the story.

They began to disperse and wander back through the trees, aiming for a nearby trail, except the man who'd killed Monique. He sat, his arms now cuffed around a tree like Leo. He looked up at her and shook his head, just as bewildered as

Damien Knight had appeared when Emma first spoke to him.

It's not like he was responsible for what he did. But Emma couldn't help hating him anyway.

The man called to them from where he sat, slumped against a tree. "Did I do...that? Please, tell me I'm not a murderer. I would never hurt anyone. I wouldn't." His gaze fixated on Monique's body as tears poured down his cheeks.

Rationality seemed to have returned to him. Emma clenched her fists, torn between reassuring him and wanting to hoist the tree branch he'd used and give him a taste of his own medicine.

Except that's not his doing, Emma girl, and you know it. This was Celeste.

In stony silence, Emma uncuffed him and pushed him to follow the others out of the woods.

"Are you okay?" Mia turned to Emma.

She hugged herself. "No. We just lost the one person who was fiercely and definitely on our side. Now that she's gone, so is her protection."

Maybe that was part of why Emma felt so empty. Because the protective spell—the last spell—was gone.

But the loss felt deeper.

I'm hollowed out. Tired, hollowed out, and all but done. If Mom was ever going to show up and help, this would be the time.

Emma knew that wouldn't happen. If her mom hadn't been able to appear by now, Monique's death wouldn't make much of a difference.

Leo appeared at her side. He knelt across from her, staring down at Monique, holding the cuffs in one hand and his keys in the other.

"Got them out of my pocket with some clever stretching."

"Really, Leo?" Mia crouched on the ground beside him, pursing her lips in disapproval.

Last Spell 227

"Okay, no. Not really. They fell out, and I wiggled around the tree so I could pick them up. Thanks for cuffing me, though."

Emma looked him straight in the eyes. "What would've happened if I hadn't cuffed you to that tree? Or taken your gun?"

Leo didn't seem to have an answer. Emma wilted to the ground beside Monique's body. She'd never felt this hopeless before, but seeing Mia and Leo lose themselves to Celeste's power had broken something within her.

Even more than Oren's death had torn at her soul, seeing her friends work against her had ruined any faith she might've had that they'd come out on top. Salem would never be the same again, and if Celeste managed to branch out to other cities, using her power to tear apart families and neighborhoods, Emma couldn't imagine what that looked like for their future.

They couldn't keep chasing her forever, but they couldn't let her escape under any circumstances. The consequences were too dire.

But she'd nearly lost her friends, her chosen family, already. Could she really ask them to go with her?

"We barely escaped the fire earlier. Any one of us could've been killed at any number of points today. There's no way of knowing if Jacinda or Vance is safe. This is such a mess." Her throat seized, tight and unyielding, as if locked in a silent scream.

"What are you saying?" Mia's voice sounded choked.

She massaged the base of her neck to loosen it enough to explain. "I'm saying you two don't have to help me anymore. Go to town, try to get things under control. I can't...I can't lose you two. My mom is gone, Monique is gone..."

She simply couldn't continue.

Leo stood, moved around Monique's body, and knelt

beside Emma, putting one hand on her shoulder. She leaned into it, thankful for the sudden contact. His hand was warm and solid, and as unmoored as she was at the moment, that alone was something.

"Emma, I…" He faltered but gripped her shoulder and went on. "Monique would want us to keep fighting. All of us. Official case or not…people still need our help, and Celeste has to be stopped, one way or another. You can't do it alone."

Emma met Leo's intense gaze.

"We don't want to lose you either. All for one, right?"

"One for all…" Emma didn't know if she fully believed the words, but saying them helped.

Her agreement seemed to spur Leo on as well. "Okay, we know she's nearby, and we're the only ones in a position to put an end to the madness she's causing. This isn't just another job. It's a mission we can't give up on. The alternative is too bleak."

The hopelessness in Emma's gut diminished, if only by a hair. This was progress, or something like it. Leo was clearly Leo again.

"I haven't asked how the two of you feel." She examined Mia, searching for any remaining sign of Celeste Foss's influence. "Are you clearheaded? If I have to go on alone to try to go after her, I—"

"I'm fine." Mia rubbed her forehead with a slight frown. "The truth is, I feel more clearheaded than I have all day. Maybe since we've reached Salem."

Leo's lip twisted. "Monique said the protection would die with her, but I think she must've done something before we lost her. I never heard her stop chanting until she collapsed."

Emma stretched her fingers, flexing her hands and then the muscles in her back. She thought back to the determination and fight she'd seen from Monique and how she'd spoken about her love for Emma's mother. Even when the woman had been frightened for her own life, she'd done everything she could to help Emma and her friends.

Her dying breath had been expended in an effort to ensure their protection.

And she knew only one way to honor that devotion.

Emma pressed her palm to Monique's lifeless shoulder. "If you see my mom, tell her I said hi." She shoved herself to her feet, rising between her two friends and allowing herself one final look upon the body of her mother's old friend. "And tell her Celeste isn't getting away with what she's done."

35

Emma had returned Mia's and Leo's guns to them. She held on to the extra, but none of Celeste's puppets appeared to impede them.

She and Leo reached the greenbelt entrance and found a pair of police cruisers already there, officers interviewing some of the people who'd staggered down from the hilltop.

A few were in cuffs. Others stood in a group as an officer reminded them all about the shelter-in-place order.

After giving their own statements, describing where Monique's body would be found, Emma surrendered the gun Celeste had given Leo. A uniformed officer accepted it, and she asked him about conditions in Salem. "Any change, or is it still Armageddon?"

"It's getting quieter, I'd say. It's like the city finally got Chief Peterson's memo. Mostly, we're hearing about folks turning themselves in or offering to help clean up." He jerked his head toward his car. "Like this guy."

Monique's killer sat in the back of a cruiser, crying and mumbling about how he would never kill anyone.

Emma wanted to tell them what they were really up

against, and at the same time, wanted to keep the information entirely to herself. She almost wished she'd come alone, so that neither Mia nor Leo would've been placed in danger.

Excusing herself without explanation, she met up with Leo on the path into the woods. They led the M.E. and her team to Monique.

Together, the group of them hurried through the forest and found Mia still on the hilltop, standing vigil over Monique. As a group, they stood to the side and let the team do their work. Once they'd finished, they rolled Monique into a black body bag and performed a two-person carry, which was easier on this terrain than the use of a gurney.

Emma clutched at her sense of calm as she breathed deep and worked to remind herself of what they were fighting for. And who.

She aimed a finger at the smaller of the two boulders. "Leo, when you were…leaving, after Celeste pulled you into the Other, you saw those stones, right?"

"Yeah. And there's a trail on the other side, at the bottom of this hill. It leads through the woods to some kind of circle of trees."

"Like the Place of Moonlight?"

He nodded. "When I saw her, she was standing in the middle of the circle. But the trees were taller." He tilted his head. "And I remember hearing water."

"Like a creek or stream?"

"Not running water, no. More like a tide lapping at a shore. And I kept picturing the color blue. Lots of it. Has to be Lorn Meadow."

"Why aren't we running into any of her soldiers?" Mia had stepped back to watch the woods behind them. "Shouldn't they still be coming after us if we're basically on her doorstep?"

Emma let out a breath. "My guess is she exhausted whatever store of energy or ability she'd built up. Taking out Monique must've drained her somehow. This is the time to take her down. We may never get a better chance."

"Let's get this done." Leo joined Mia in pacing the hilltop, scanning around them.

Emma nodded and stepped past him and Mia to lead the way around the boulders and down the hillside to the forest below.

As they reached the lower elevation, the cold of the Other greeted her.

Oren stood near a tree. He wore a smile and waved them on, toward a trail that clearly pierced the thick woods. Emma wanted so badly to reach for him, but his face was set like stone, and his white eyes wouldn't even shift to meet hers.

He merely held out a hand, pointing them onward.

The three of them continued into the trees until the familiar lap of a lakeshore tide echoed back to them. She aimed her trajectory in that direction, feeling Leo and Mia shift behind her.

You can do this, Emma Last. You can.

The words might've come from Oren, or they might've been her own, or even her mother's, or Monique's. No matter. Emma let them drive her forward.

Around her, familiar, white-eyed faces appeared. The children they'd lost in the opera house tunnels, bled out and left to die. Even the circus performers from her and Mia and Leo's first case together, when all this had started for her. The trapeze artist and the bodybuilder nodded at her, holding out hands just as Oren had done, as if showing her the way. Her heart pounded with the emotion of seeing all those victims again, from knowing they were thanking her in perhaps the only way they could.

When Ned Logan appeared, walking briefly beside Mia,

Emma smiled in his direction, no longer surprised. The whole of the Other was invested in this fight.

They know this is a fight I need to win. For everyone.

She could feel it now—the power of this place. Power could run both ways. If Celeste could draw on it, Emma had no reason to believe that she couldn't do so as well.

Only, she would use it for good. And perhaps her friends in the Other would even be able to use it on her behalf.

Her vision fogged, going gray around the edges and blurring against the trees, but even as her step faltered, and she felt a dragging weight of doubt fill her mind, a hand came down on her shoulder from behind. Instantly, her strength and resolve came back.

She looked over to see Leo's smiling face. And then Mia gripped her arm, pushing her on between them.

Oren's voice echoed from behind her, vibrating in the air, and the quick jerk of Leo's hand against her shoulder told her he'd heard it too.

"You can hear him?"

Leo nodded. "Not until I put my hand on your shoulder. Then I could hear all of them. Even Ned."

Mia clutched her upper arm tighter. "Ned's here?"

"Yes, he's pointing us in the right direction."

From behind her, Oren's voice continued urging them forward. "Stay centered, Emma. You're strong. You've always been strong. Just watch out."

"He's right." Leo moved faster to match Emma's speeding pace. "Don't forget that."

Emma nodded, biting her lip to curb her urge to respond to either Oren or Leo. She could feel the mental fog battering at her mind again, attempting to make her doubt herself as it blurred the edges of the path before her, but she wouldn't allow it. Not when her friends were counting on her.

The air grew colder, thicker, and ghosts appeared at the

sides of the path. Some echoed Oren's confidence. Others only watched. Emma's skin chilled even as she pressed on, but whether the edge of the path blurred or remained steady ahead, she forced herself to continue without faltering again, counting on Leo's and Mia's hands to keep her centered on the pathway they needed to follow.

She saw the lakeshore now, through the trees.

The sound of water cresting against a shoreline blended with a sudden gust of wind that shook the leaves and whistled through the air.

The whistling grew heavier, deeper, until all Emma heard was the hungry baying of a wolf. They'd found Celeste even before they saw her.

She stood waiting in the center of a ring of trees bordering a wide peninsula. Their trunks were thick and tall, rising high overhead into a canopy that concealed most of the early evening sunlight. This was Lorn Meadow, cradled inside lots of crystal-blue water.

She opened her mouth and let out another lupine howl that broke off into delighted laughter. "At last, Emma. I will take back what Gina stole from me."

Emma stepped steadily toward Celeste, focused on only her. By the time she stopped and felt for her friends, needing to know they were still by her side, they'd vanished.

Nothing but wisps of Other mist swirled about where they'd flanked her. She spun in a circle to scan the area. Nothing.

Celeste's growling laughter pulled her back to the scene in front of her. "That's right, my girl. We're in the Other, and your friends, I'm sorry to say, were not invited." The woman stood there, still in her uniform with her weapon holstered on her hip. A bulletproof vest peeked from beneath the collar of her shirt. "Nobody else can help you now, but I'll give you the chance Gina never gave me."

"You're out of control and off your rocker, Celeste. My mom never did anything to hurt you. Never took anything of yours that you need to get back." Emma planted her feet, squarely facing Celeste. "The only thing she did was choose to live her life as she saw fit. That's called freedom, and it's something you've stolen from countless people. You're the thief."

Celeste hovered her hand above her service weapon. "Gina took my family when she chose you over me. Call it whatever you want. Gina could've upheld our pact and been standing here beside me right now. Instead, I'm alone." A small, ironic chuckle floated out of Celeste's mouth. "But you're alone, too, aren't you, my girl?"

Emma's patience had reached its limit. The woman had caused more damage and loss of life in one week than all the killers Emma had helped bring down since her career began. "This ends now. Stand down and place your hands in the air." She reached for her weapon.

Celeste put up one hand, beckoning her to wait. "Like I said, my girl. You'll get your chance, which is more than you deserve. But unlike your mother, I still believe in keeping promises I've made. You're welcome to arrest me and take me in." Her lips curled into a grin. "If you can."

36

Emma pulled her gun free and aimed it at the woman. "Last time, Celeste Foss. Stand down. Place both hands in the air and get on your knees."

Celeste held herself in a relaxed posture. Her hand hovered above her weapon, but it was loose, not tensed as if ready to draw. "I don't think so." In a motion so swift she blurred in action, Celeste whipped her weapon from her holster and aimed at the place where Leo had been standing.

In another blink, she vanished.

Emma stepped back again and again until she finally turned and hustled to the edge of the trees ringing Celeste's sanctuary, feeling the wispy tendrils of Other mist against her skin, as ghosts swam in and out of her periphery.

Where the hell did she go?

Taking a deep breath, Emma focused on what she knew was real. The scent of the trees, the sound of the lakeshore. Leo's voice.

"Emma! Where are you?"

Leo?

The sound seemed to come from the center of the circle,

where Celeste had been standing. Emma charged back to that spot and instantly experienced a shock of chill against her neck. She spun around and ran back out to the circle's edge and stood there to see the evening sun cutting through the trees and shining directly on her.

Leo whispered again. "Where…?"

She'd returned to the living world.

The sound of gunshots cut through the trees. Leo's voice rang out. "Dammit, Emma! Where are you?"

He and Mia were in a shoot-out. It had to be Celeste, but where was she?

"Here! I'm here! I'm coming!" She raced into the woods in the direction of their voices, looking for cover and scanning the forest for Celeste. She couldn't see the woman anywhere.

But Oren was there. "She's moving between both places, Emma. You can use the sanctuary to do that too. You have to center yourself."

Pulling up beside a thick tree, Emma counted down from five to calm her breathing. Peering through the tree trunks, she saw Leo and Mia, both still okay. The shooting had stopped, and they'd both taken cover behind a large tree standing several feet outside Celeste's sanctuary. They couldn't see her, but Emma guessed Celeste had a clear sight line to her friends.

"This isn't going to end the way you think it will, Celeste! Drop your weapon and come out with your hands in the air!" Leo's voice echoed around them, only to be met by Celeste's mocking laughter.

"Oh, my boy, what you *don't* know about this situation could fill an encyclopedia."

A shot rang out, and Mia shrieked. She quickly confirmed she wasn't hit, though. "I'm fine. Where the hell did Emma go? Do you see her?"

Emma still couldn't get a line of sight on Celeste, but she

wasn't sure she wanted Leo or Mia to know where she was, so she stayed put.

Calling their attention to her might get them to move into Celeste's line of fire. If Celeste knew she'd followed her from the Other back into the real world, the woman might be waiting for Emma to act and using Leo and Mia as bait.

Maybe that's the way to end this. Get her back into the Other, where she can't hurt Leo and Mia. And since she seems to think this whole meadow and forest and lake belong to her...

Holding her weapon steady, Emma spun around the tree she'd been hiding behind, aiming her voice in the direction that Leo and Mia had been shooting. "Come and get me, Celeste. Leave my friends out of this."

She turned around and raced back to the circle inside the trees that formed Celeste's sanctuary, charging as fast as she could on a path toward its center.

That had to be what Oren meant. Get to the center, and I can get back into the Other.

"Come on, Celeste! You think this circle belongs to you? Well, I'm about to claim it as my own."

"How dare you!" The woman's scream of rage echoed through the trees. Emma kept running, aiming herself at the center of the circle. If she could draw Celeste out of cover, either Leo or Mia might get a shot at her.

If they missed her, and Celeste chased Emma to the circle's center, then she'd take her chances against the woman in the Other.

37

At the tree line at the edge of Lorn Meadow, Emma focused on Oren's memory. She thought of him as she'd seen him in the Other the first time he came to her.

Sitting on that bench outside the Yoga Map, with his legs taking up most of the seat, like a true manspreader.

Emma crossed into the circle toward its powerful center, hearing Celeste's angry shouts behind her. In an instant, the world changed to glaring white, and Emma could see nothing else.

Thick tendrils of dusty white smoke obscured her vision, and the chill went straight to her bones, locking her in place. She heard no sound, smelled nothing in the air, and felt no warmth or light from the sun's rays.

The pure whiteness of the world hurt her eyes, and Emma couldn't even guess as to whether she might be in some prison inside Celeste's mind or in the Other. Things had really gone off the rails since entering Salem. Her understanding of the real world and the Other had shot to new heights, so anything was possible.

"It's just the two of us now." Celeste stepped out of a fog of powder-white smoke, her long silver hair, like another layer of atmosphere, tangled over her shoulders like fur.

Emma swallowed her fear on seeing the woman's glowing chestnut eyes.

"Just the two of us. And you'll never defeat me here, in *my* sanctuary."

"You're wrong, Celeste." The voice came from behind Emma.

She dared not turn, but there was no need. Monique's ghost had been the one to speak, and her voice was just as solid and clear as her own thoughts.

But when her mother's voice echoed Monique's words, Emma had to turn. She watched as the two ghosts emerged from the swirling mist. Monique looked like a reenergized, well-rested version of herself. And her mother, well, she looked just like Emma. It was like looking in a mirror. They were the same age after all, both twenty-eight.

Emma glanced at each woman, and warmth blazed through her chest on seeing Monique "alive" in the Other and her mother—her beautiful mother—just inches from her.

With these two beloved spirits behind her, Emma faced Celeste once more.

Celeste's eyes opened wide as the two women came closer, one on either side of Emma.

"It's not possible you're here. That either of you are here!" Celeste glared at her old friends before looking into the whiteness above them, as if searching for explanation. "It's not possible. This sanctuary is mine. I claimed this place as my own!"

Gina stepped forward with Monique, putting themselves between Emma and Celeste. "Nothing you've attempted could ever succeed against love. You should've known that."

Celeste snarled. "You sound like you always did, Gina, leaning on fantasies like 'promises' and 'love.' What do you know about either of them? You broke every promise you made to me, and you gave your love away to the first pretty rich boy to catch your eye."

Emma's skin chilled with the crackling air around them as she listened to the three old friends confront one another after so many years apart.

Reaching out a hand toward Celeste, Monique led Gina forward another step. "You don't understand. You never did. We bound ourselves to one another as a promise of support and intention. When some of our intentions changed, the nature of our bond may've changed, but that bond still remained. You being here, in this space you call a sanctuary, means we can also be here."

Emma's mother glanced over her shoulder and locked eyes with her, and Emma experienced a surge of love so strong, as if it were making up for a lifetime of missed memories.

Her mother turned back to Celeste. "We can be here to oppose you and to support my daughter."

Without hesitation, Celeste raised her weapon and fired at Emma.

Emma stared in disbelief as the bullets came to a stop in front of her chest and dropped. She flinched backward, but Monique cast her a calming smile. "You're protected here, Emma dear." Her smile drooped into a frown. "Sadly, you're protected by the same pact protecting Celeste."

Two more gunshots rang out, and Emma instinctively dodged to the side before pausing as she watched the bullets again slow, stop, and fall to the ground.

Celeste screamed. "Impossible! They've been instructed to find their target!" She took a step toward the center of the circle, where she'd been standing when Emma first entered the space.

"You mustn't let her reach the center point, Emma." Her mother urged her forward. "Go, claim it yourself, or she'll be free to move out of the Other, where we cannot help you."

Emma charged for the patch of earth at the circle's center point as Celeste made her own mad run for it. They'd reach it at the same time, but at least that meant she could exit along with the other woman.

With several strides to go, Emma's mother and Monique began speaking, their voices raised loud and clear. "We reject our sisterhood, Celeste Foss. We reject our sisterhood and name you a betrayer."

Celeste's face burned with rage as she sprinted for the center, but as the final words left Monique's and Gina's lips, Emma watched as a change came over her opponent.

Fury turned to disgust and finally shifted into grim resignation. Celeste stopped running and brought her weapon up at Emma. "Gloves are off now, my girl. And so are the shields. For me and for you."

Celeste fired, and a bullet zipped around Emma's head with a trailing cold wind, icier even than the Other mists surrounding her.

Emma flinched and took off at a run, mostly out of instinct—harder to hit a moving target.

The other woman fired again. And again. Each shot missed, but just barely, and each time, Celeste's face grew more twisted with rage as she screamed in frustration and fury. "Damn you, Gina! You lying bitch, you're still protecting her!"

Gina's calm voice rang out from the edge of the circle. "Of course I am."

Another bullet flew past Emma's head, sending a deep chill tugging across her brow. Celeste roared and charged.

Emma had her own weapon up and sent a shot in Celeste's direction. As the bullet left the gun, she zigzagged, came to a stop, pivoted, and fired again.

The shot hit Celeste in the stomach. Her vest took the brunt of the blow, but she still went down, clutching at her midsection. Emma charged in her direction, weapon still up and aiming at her center mass.

Celeste whimpered and sat halfway up. "This isn't done, Emma Last." She coughed to catch her breath. "When your sister learns of what you've done to me, she will find you, and she will end you."

Celeste lifted her gun.

With a strangled cry, Emma fired a final time, striking the woman between the eyes and sending her onto her back.

She was dead.

In the aftermath of the firefight, the silence seemed to stretch on forever. Emma wondered if she'd be trapped here, in the swirling wisps and quiet. For a moment, she thought she might be dead too.

It was so, so quiet.

Tears burned hot against the backs of Emma's eyelids as the warmth of her mother's and Monique's hands rested above her shoulders. "It's over, Emma. You've done it, and we are now free."

Emma put a hand up, wanting so badly to feel her mother's skin against her own, but her ghostly presence wasn't something Emma could touch. Her mother's hand wasn't really touching her shoulder but hovered there like a butterfly over a stalk of lavender.

"Mom, what did she mean? Do I have a sister?"

"I have no idea what she meant." Her mother's ghost stared down at her former friend. "Celeste has always played mind games."

Emma wanted so desperately to believe her. But

something in Celeste's voice had sounded so true, so honest, even if it was spoken with such intense malice.

She turned to see a hint of the blue behind her mother's ghostly white eyes.

The smile on her face offered the same image Emma had looked at in pictures every morning and night for as long as she could remember.

The pain began to ebb, pulling away from her, and some of the tension left her body. "Mom…"

Her mother smiled, her lips pressed together tightly, as if holding back a sob.

There was so much Emma wanted to ask her. To tell her.

"I'm so proud of you, Emma. So proud."

Emma closed her eyes, unable to stop herself, and the Other blazed around her so that her whole body went cold and then hot. A fog pressed against her mind again—though it disappeared as fast as it had come.

Gasping, Emma relaxed and met her mother's eyes. "Thank you." She looked at Monique. "Both of you. I think I'll be okay. I will, I mean…I think I will. Without you."

"We will always be with you." Her mother's hand came to her cheek, and warmth flooded Emma's face.

Her mother reached for Monique, and the two clasped hands.

"Goodbye, my love." She winked.

Both women shimmered in the air in front of her before vanishing without a trace.

And Emma was alone.

She had ended a fight that had begun before she was even born and brought closure to the one person she'd never before been able to speak to, much less help.

Taking a deep, calming breath, just as Oren always encouraged her to do in his yoga classes, Emma prepared to step out of the Other. It was time to go back to the people still with her. The people she could still help.

Emma released her breath and walked to Celeste's body.

Then she dragged her to the center of her sanctuary. With slow, heavy steps, Emma brought them both back into her own world.

38

Emma opened her eyes to find Mia and Leo off in the distance, weaving between trees.

"Emma? Emma, are you okay? What happened?" Leo began running toward her, holstering his weapon as he came. Mia did the same right behind him. Neither was steady on their feet, but they joined her by Celeste's body and scanned the area in all directions, as if expecting possessed suburbanites or ghosts to suddenly appear and start attacking them.

Breathing deeply, Emma swallowed down a wave of fatigue. She glanced at Celeste's body one more time, assuring herself she was dead.

She explained to her friends about being in the Other with Celeste, how the woman had vanished from it initially to attack the two of them back in the real world, and how Emma lured her back to the Other for their showdown.

"That's how she did it." Leo shook his head. "She was inside the circle of trees one minute, and then gone. Both of you just winked out like lights. But then the next thing we knew, she's popping off at us from outside the circle and hiding behind trees."

Mia picked up the story. "And then you showed up again. We had no idea where you'd gone. And then, bam, you were back."

"I was in the Other, with her, somehow. But it wasn't like when Monique did that to me. It felt smoother. Seamless, really." Emma looked back to the spot where she'd crossed over to the Other. "I walked right into it as I approached Celeste in the center point of the circle. Then I could go in and out at will, once I got it. Oren helped me understand how it worked, to be honest. I can still feel the power of this circle, but it's waning."

Emma described how Celeste's bullets refused to hit her. And how her mother and Monique appeared to help. How she finally took Celeste down.

When she'd finished the tale, the adrenaline from the fight was replaced with a nervous tension. Unwilling to put it off any longer, Emma gazed at her friends. "I need to tell you something."

She had no sister as far as she knew, so the message felt all the stranger as she relayed it. But, word for word, she shared what Celeste had said with her dying breath.

"When your sister learns of what you've done to me...she will find you, and she will end you."

Shell-shocked, Mia only stared for a minute. "I don't understand."

Emma tore her fingers through her hair, exhaling hard with frustration. "I don't either."

"She must've been lying." Leo frowned, gazing down at Celeste's body. "She must've been hoping to torment you from beyond the grave because she could do nothing else to hurt you."

That made sense, but Emma couldn't help shaking her head. "I don't know. She sounded like she was telling the truth. And I'm not sure...I'm not sure she could've lied at that point, in the place she was in. She'd lost so much by then."

"But why?" Mia scowled. "I mean, even if you have a sister, why would she align herself with Celeste rather than you and your mother?" She chewed her lip. "Unless we were right, and Celeste did have a child of her own, one she lost, and 'sister' is being used figuratively."

Emma thought of that pink bedroom in Celeste's burned-up home. She thought of the discussion she'd had with Leo and Mia. Had the woman had a miscarriage? Her mother or Monique might have never known about that. If so, was she talking about the spirit of an unborn child that was coming for Emma to avenge her mother?

Emma sighed, unable to take her eyes from the dead witch who'd done so much damage. "I guess it's possible there's a baby or young ghost out there who would like nothing more than to see me dead because I just killed her mother."

Mia sighed. "I would think that baby would be happy to finally be with her mom in the Other."

Breathing heavily, Emma shook herself back to this reality, this world. They had enough to worry about without paranoia coming into play. "Let's go back to the car and get out of here."

Leo swept some hair out of his eyes, a shaky smile on his face. "I don't think I've heard a better idea in my life."

Mia waved them back. "There's a dead police officer lying on the ground behind you. We're federal agents who swore an oath of duty and allegiance. No matter what we've seen or done today, that hasn't changed. Has it?"

"Mia's right. We're back to normal protocol now, even if this wasn't a normal case. Someone should stay here with the body, now that we're no longer in such an urgent situation." Emma hugged herself. "We can send up the alert for emergency personnel to come collect her, then come back so it's not just one person out here in the woods waiting alone."

"I'll do it." Mia waved her hands. "You and Leo have been through it today. Go hydrate, call the cavalry, and come back. Emma, maybe you should leave your weapon with me, though. I'll assume Incident Command." She pressed her lips together. "Under protocol, I should take all fired weapons, but there's nothing in the protocol that covers everything we've just seen and done."

Emma smiled for the first time in what seemed like ages. "Very true. We'll follow proper procedure once we know for sure that everything is okay outside of these woods."

Leo didn't argue as he turned back to the path. Emma cleared her gun and handed it to Mia before turning to follow him, already parsing through what she'd tell Jacinda when they reached her on the phone. Not that an explanation would be easy to come by.

The path back was easy to follow. Ghosts—Shades, she reminded herself—appeared and disappeared ahead of them, nodding at Emma and offering smiles and words of thanks.

Emma tried to meet each of their white gazes with her own, wanting to show what respect and honor she could, but her whole body ached with exhaustion and tension.

One thought kept swirling in her brain. How could her mother have given birth to a child before Emma? Surely, Monique and Celeste would've known about that.

What if the child wasn't her mother's…but her father's? Emma shook her head as if to knock the thought out of her mind. She had to stop thinking about all this.

As they neared the hillside rising up to the boulders, voices drifted down from above.

Jacinda and Vance came around the looming stones. They

all but tumbled down the hillside, as they came running so fast on spotting them.

Vance's eyes widened as he reached the bottom. "Where's Mia? Is she okay?"

"She's fine!" Emma raised her voice over his panic, but she met his eyes and willed him to believe her. "She stayed behind to control the scene, that's all."

"What scene? Where?" Vance looked back and forth between them, and Emma waited for Jacinda's nod before stepping aside and gesturing him past.

"Follow this path toward the lake. Just listen for the tide. You'll get to a dense wood, and then you'll see a circle of trees on a peninsula. You'll find her in there. One perpetrator, deceased. It was my shot. Mia established IC and has my weapon."

"Got it." Vance rushed off.

Emma turned back to face the SSA. "I can give you my statement, Jacinda."

"What about you?" Jacinda looked at Leo, and he paused.

Emma jumped in to save him. "I was the only one involved in direct confrontation on this scene. Mia and Leo received fire and returned it, but at the end, it was just me and...Detective Foss."

Jacinda's eyes widened. "What—?"

Emma put up a hand. "She was dirty, Jacinda. I can prove it. We just need to review her equipment. She was behind all the bombs in town, so she'll have a detonation device somewhere."

Jacinda raised her gaze to Emma's, flat-lipped. "It's good to know the primary culprit has been dealt with, but I hope you can explain what the hell's been happening and confirm it's over."

"It's over." Leo looked at Emma, hesitating. "Beyond that—"

Emma didn't let him get any further. Explanations could wait. "All we can confirm at the moment is that it's definitely over."

39

Emma lay in corpse pose in the middle of the park. Dawn broke over the horizon, and she welcomed the glowing light pouring over her. In the days after Salem, she'd found herself scrambling with paperwork, answering the same questions over and over during interviews, and wondering if she'd dreamed the whole thing.

Tension still stored in her muscles told her she'd done everything she remembered.

Returning to the everyday world had been surreal after being surrounded by such strange forces she couldn't hope to fully understand. It was a comfort to lay on her mat, feeling the blades of grass with her fingertips as she let her hands drift. The earth beneath her was solid. In fact, she was pretty sure there was a rock under her left hip.

She wished her mind felt centered.

In a million ways, she'd learned how lucky she was. Her mother loved her. She had friends who supported her and would literally go to other worlds and back for her. They'd face death with her.

But she kept hearing Celeste's voice, niggling at the back of her mind.

"When your sister learns of what you've done to me, she will find you, and she will end you."

Despite her mother's reassurance that Celeste played mind games, Emma couldn't shake the sense that Celeste was telling the truth.

It was the bedroom in Celeste's house that clinched the probable truth for Emma.

Why was there a bedroom in Celeste's house that looked like it belonged to a teenage girl? Admittedly, the room didn't appear to have been lived in for a while. But it clearly didn't belong to Celeste either. Someone else lived in that house. A girl someone.

A sister, though?

"It's not over." She whispered the words into the warming morning air. No matter how much she might wish it otherwise, something else was coming.

Emma closed her eyes against the sun, which was now glaring at her. It was time to let these thoughts go and get back to work.

She stood and returned to her apartment. Mrs. Kellerly didn't bother her this morning, and she showered in peace. After a quick cup of coffee and a short, traffic-free drive, she was at the office, ready to go.

Emma made it all the way to the chair at her desk before Jacinda called to her from the conference room.

"Emma? Can you join us?"

Even though she was no longer in middle school, Jacinda's tone made Emma's gut clench as if she were being called to the principal's office. After all the interviews and explanations she and Leo and Mia had given, she didn't think she had the energy to create any more vague-but-plausible answers.

The main thrust of the cover story actually centered on the truth. Detective Celeste Foss had orchestrated terrorist action on Salem. She had stolen ammunition and explosives from the department armory and unleashed a reign of random attacks. Emma had told a reporter, *"Her motives are unclear at this time and may be related to a psychological break."*

They'd managed to avoid any mention of the supernatural.

Still, she took a deep breath and headed over to the conference room.

She reached the doorway and froze. Special Agent Denae Monroe sat with Jacinda at the table. It had been a while since Denae had been in the office. In fact, Emma was under the impression that Danae was taking an extended leave after being critically shot during a sting operation on a meth developer. She was lucky to be alive.

Emma knew that, because she'd seen Denae in the Other, flickering in and out of life.

A smile so big it hurt took over Emma's face. "Denae, I'm—"

"Please sit down, Agent Last." Jacinda gestured toward a chair. "We need to sort something out."

Emma glanced from Jacinda to Denae. Her fellow agents' faces were more serious than she'd ever seen. Her stomach swooped.

Denae met her gaze. "It's about the ghosts."

The End
To be continued...

Thank you for reading.
All of Emma Last series books can be found on Amazon.

ACKNOWLEDGMENTS

The past few years have been a whirlwind of change, both personally and professionally, and I find myself at a loss for the right words to express my profound gratitude to those who have supported me on this remarkable journey. Yet, I am compelled to try.

To my sons, whose unwavering support has been my bedrock, granting me the time and energy to transform my darkest thoughts into words on paper. Your steadfast belief in me has never faltered, and watching each of you grow, welcoming the wonderful daughters you've brought into our family, has been a source of immense pride and joy.

Embarking on the dual role of both author and publisher has been an exhilarating, albeit challenging, adventure. Transitioning from the solitude of writing to the dynamic world of publishing has opened new horizons for me, and I'm deeply grateful for the opportunity to share my work directly with you, the readers.

I extend my heartfelt thanks to the entire team at Mary Stone Publishing, the same dedicated group who first recognized my potential as an indie author years ago. Your collective efforts, from the editors whose skillful hands have polished my words to the designers, marketers, and support staff who breathe life into these books, have been instrumental in resonating deeply with our readers. Each of you plays a crucial role in this journey, not only nurturing my growth but also ensuring that every story reaches its full potential. Your dedication, creativity, and finesse have been nothing short of invaluable.

However, my deepest gratitude is reserved for you, my beloved readers. You ventured off the beaten path of traditional publishing to embrace my work, investing your most precious asset—your time. It is my sincerest hope that this book has enriched that time, leaving you with memories that linger long after the last page is turned.

With all my love and heartfelt appreciation,

Mary

ABOUT THE AUTHOR

Nestled in the serene Blue Ridge Mountains of East Tennessee, Mary Stone crafts her stories surrounded by the natural beauty that inspires her. What was once a home filled with the lively energy of her sons has now become a peaceful writer's retreat, shared with cherished pets and the vivid characters of her imagination.

As her sons grew and welcomed wonderful daughters-in-law into the family, Mary's life entered a quieter phase, rich with opportunities for deep creative focus. In this tranquil environment, she weaves tales of courage, resilience, and intrigue, each story a testament to her evolving journey as a writer.

From childhood fears of shadowy figures under the bed to a profound understanding of humanity's real-life villains, Mary's style has been shaped by the realization that the most complex antagonists often hide in plain sight. Her writing is characterized by strong, multifaceted heroines who defy traditional roles, standing as equals among their peers in a world of suspense and danger.

Mary's career has blossomed from being a solitary author to establishing her own publishing house—a significant milestone that marks her growth in the literary world. This expansion is not just a personal achievement but a reflection of her commitment to bring thrilling and thought-provoking stories to a wider audience. As an author and publisher, Mary continues to challenge the conventions of the thriller genre, inviting readers into gripping tales filled with serial killers, astute FBI agents, and intrepid heroines who confront peril with unflinching bravery.

Each new story from Mary's pen—or her publishing house—is a pledge to captivate, thrill, and inspire, continuing the legacy of the imaginative little girl who once found wonder and mystery in the shadows.

Discover more about Mary Stone on her website.
www.authormarystone.com

Printed in Great Britain
by Amazon